# THE LAST CHRISTMAS TREE

## MIRACLES HAPPEN

INSPIRED BY A TRUE STORY

# LANDRIA ONKKA

outskirtspress

DENVER, COLORADO

Outskirts Press, Inc.
http://www.outskirtspress.com

ISBN: 978-1-4787-4001-8

Outskirts Press and the "OP" logo are trademarks belonging to Outskirts Press, Inc.

PRINTED IN THE UNITED STATES OF AMERICA

Everyone likes a story with a happy ending. I know that I do. When that ending includes a miracle, it offers hope that there may be one in store for all of us, no matter what our status in this world. Miracles take many forms. Sometimes they are blatant and other times it isn't until much later that we realize one had occurred. When we are open to the possibilities, we are no longer surprised at the miraculous and are able to embrace all that life has to offer. We are all exceptional and capable of experiencing miracles in our lives at any moment. What a better time for one than at Christmas. This is one of those stories. Miracles happen. Believe.

This story is dedicated to my parents, Don and Sandra who always supported and believed in me, and my pup Skeezer, all of whom I lost in a short period. Thank you Mom for being my editor although you never got to read the final draft, and to my Dad who allowed me to pursue my dreams. I miss and love all of you so much.

# Contents

## Chapter One

# Working Too Much

"Doug! Stop it! You're purposely trying to kick it into the street," young Sarah shouts pushing messy, blond locks off of her face as she runs. Her younger brother is pleased with his powerful shot that places the soccer ball at the edge of the curb.

Shafts of sunlight, thick with the wet Georgia air look like heavy beams of fog. Flush faced southern ladies rock on big wooden porches, gossiping and cooling off with sweet tea and whispering overhead fans. A baseball game blasts from an antiquated radio in a garage, circled by weathered gentlemen sitting on lawn chairs.

"Run faster!" Doug wrinkles his freckled face as Sarah kicks the ball back to her brother. A young woman in her 20's sits on her front porch steps directly across the street. Her head hangs as she blankly stares at the ground.

Doug gives the ball an extra hard kick, surprising himself with the overly aggressive shot. He gasps as it sails into the street and bounces, unimpeded onto the woman's front lawn.

"Doug! I told you!" Sarah swiftly runs after it as it finds a home in a bed of Begonias only a few feet from the woman. Her head suddenly jerks up, revealing a face of rage.

"I told you kids to stay off my lawn! You don't have any respect! Get that ball out of my flowers and stay in your own yard!" she screams, disturbing the peaceful afternoon atmosphere and grabbing the attention of everyone within ear shot.

Sarah quickly plucks the ball out of the flower bed and runs as fast as she can back to the safety of her own yard. Doug has already scrambled up the porch steps, slamming the screen door behind him, disregarding his sister who is fast on his tail. The children run through the living room, past the dining room and into a bright kitchen skidding and almost colliding with their mother who is making sandwiches.

"Mom, the crazy lady yelled at us!" Doug shouts, panting out of breath.

"Well what did you two do to upset her?" she calmly asks as she continues her work.

The children shrug their shoulders. "Just kicked the ball and it accidentally rolled on her lawn, honest! We didn't mean it!" Doug explains quickly, still gasping.

"OK, you two. That's fine. It was an accident. You can relax now. You know not to disturb her, and you know she isn't crazy. I don't want to hear that word come out of your mouths again. Mrs. Landis is sad and it is none of our business. Be respectful of our neighbor please, and try to be more careful," she replies.

"Sarah did it, Mom," Doug tattles. Sarah gives him an angry stare.

"Well she sure is sad *a lot*, and she is *mean*!" Sarah replies, as she walks to the living room window. She spots the young woman who stands up, head hanging, and slowly walks back into her home.

Their mother places the sandwiches on the dining room table. "Sarah, please forget about our neighbor's troubles for now. Wash your hands and come eat your lunch."

Sarah continues to stare out the window, watching as the neighbor slams her front door then closes heavy curtains that block out the bright, Georgia sun.

"Sarah, now go wash your hands like I asked and come eat your lunch. Sarah! Sarah! Are you coming? Sarah?"

Sarah's eyes pop open and she jerks her head up to see attorney William Gants leaning over her. "Sarah! Are you coming? Sarah?" he raises his voice until he sees that Sarah begins to respond. "Geez, I thought you finally collapsed from exhaustion. Counselor, you need to get more sleep. Your case is up shortly. You need to get to the courthouse!"

"Oh my gosh!" Sarah looks around the room blinking as she fights to focus her eyes, realizing where she is. A pile of books and stack of papers are strewn across a long table in the research room at her law office.

"Wow, I was having an odd dream. I was a kid, playing kickball with my brother and," William gives her an odd look. "I think you're right, Will. I need more sleep. I can't believe I nodded off like that in the middle of researching." She shakes her numb arm, trying to get the blood circulating. "How embarrassing. I hope I didn't drool!" Sarah begins to collect her papers.

"I don't know how you can sleep propped on your hand like that," William pauses and looks off in the distance, reminiscing. "My signature sleep pose was the two handed head rest," he smiles. "I'd put a book under my face in the library so that people would think that I was reading. I was quite good at it and could sleep for as long as an hour." He watches Sarah rub her arm. "Not as likely to lose blood flow. You should try it some time."

"I'll have to remember that," Sarah smiles as she continues to quickly organize the mountain of documents. "Will, thanks for hunting me down." Sarah stuffs everything in her briefcase, grabs her coat, and heads for the door.

"Not a problem Sarah," William replies. "Good luck with your case!"

*Chapter Two*

# The Good Attorney

"Hello there Miss Sarah!" A burley worker waves a muscle bound arm wrapped with multiple strings of colored bulbs that swing as he balances on the top of a tall ladder partially buried in a massive fir tree. "Up here!" he yells to the pretty blond running down the sidewalk below. Sarah's high heel catches in a crack and yanks off of her foot. She stumbles forward, hopping on one leg and turns back to reclaim the rebellious stiletto.

"Andy!" Sarah struggles to slip back into the shoe. She yanks a handful of curls back from her face to look up, squinting to block the final rays of sun that pierce over the roof of the courthouse. "Getting our tree ready so soon? " Sarah continues to wiggle back into her shoe.

"Another glorious Christmas is upon us, Miss Sarah!" he happily announces.

"Well, I am glad that you are so enthusiastic, but be careful up there! I am sure that Marla would like to have you home in one piece for Christmas," Sarah nervously watches him teeter on the top ladder step.

"You know I will, Miss Sarah. I reckon Marla wouldn't want to raise five kids on her own. But I don't plan on leaving this earth by falling off of a ladder! I'm a pro at this. You know, it's my tenth year decorating the courthouse tree and she gets bigger and more beautiful every year, don't you think?" he smiles.

"I hope you are talking about that tree and not your darling wife!" Sarah responds. Andy belts out a huge laugh, shaking the ladder. "Ten years, ugh," Sarah says under her breath, realizing that she had witnessed the display and dismantling of all ten of those trees. She was no longer the young attorney on the scene.

"We appreciate your handiwork, Andy," she quickly refocuses and hustles up the stone steps of the stately building, struggling to open the heavy door.

"Sarah! There you are! Geez, do you know what time it is?" A tall lanky attorney approaches, attempting to keep up with her as she sprints down the hall packed with plaintiffs and defendants.

"Yes, Bob. I am well aware that I am late," she responds, maintaining her pace.

"Your client is already in the courtroom," he announces.

"I'm doing my best, Bob," Sarah navigates her way to her favorite clerk, Claire, perched behind a counter. Claire with the kind, Aunt Bea face and demeanor was always a welcome sight. Sarah pushes her way to the counter and turns to face her colleague. "Bob, I've got this, really." Bob hesitates then frowns. "I mean it. Now go," Sarah pats him on his back, turns and signs in.

Bob shakes his head. "O.K., but I think you are taking on too much, Sarah. Your future partner position is well secured, you know. You don't have to prove yourself by trying to take on every case," he continues down the corridor, stops and turns around. "And Sarah," he makes sure he has her attention, "You look like hell. Get some sleep."

"Thanks Bob. I'll give it consideration," Sarah responds sarcastically.

"Hello Counselor. Cutting it a bit close, aren't we?" Claire twirls in her chair, rolls to a pile of files and rolls back to the counter with them. Her cheeks are full and pink, and her eyes sparkle. "You are scheduled for courtroom C and I believe your case is up . . . now." Claire gives an exaggerated look at the large wall clock behind her, leans forward and crooks her finger to draw Sarah in closer. "You might want to hustle, Sarah. Judge Conner is not in a very good mood today and you know he doesn't tolerate tardiness," she whispers.

"Thanks for the 'heads up' Claire." Sarah scoops up the papers before hustling down the hall.

"And Sarah," Claire is careful to keep her voice low, "Bob's right. Get some sleep. You look exhausted!"

Sarah gives Claire a nod and makes her way to her appointment. She stops abruptly at the courtroom door takes a deep breath, and straightens her suit jacket before entering. Sarah spots her client, a poorly dressed and unshaven, middle aged man. His face brightens at the sight of her. She quietly slides in next to him on the bench and gives his arm a comforting squeeze.

Judge Conner resides at the front of the courtroom. A short, portly man, he takes up every inch of his large, wooden chair. A long time friend of Sarah's family, he provided much guidance through-out her legal studies and career. Judge Conner means business, but Sarah quickly learned that beneath the tough exterior was a kind man who extended himself to anyone in need. She often counted on that kindness, although it had its limits when it came to legal matters.

Sarah's quiet entrance did not go unnoticed. "Ms. Wright, how nice of you to join us. Perhaps we can begin proceedings." The Judge gives her a stern look. "That is if you are ready."

"Your Honor, I apologize for the delay." Sarah quickly walks to the front of the room and clears her throat. "Mr. Roberts, my client," she gestures to her client sitting on the bench, "would like to submit a plea of 'guilty' to the charge of theft. Mr. Roberts would like to address the court on his own behalf in regard to this offense." Sarah motions for the defendant to join her.

"Mr. Roberts, approach the bench, please," the Judge firmly orders. The defendant slowly moves out of his seat making his way to the front of the courtroom and begins to mumble. "Speak up, Mr. Roberts," the Judge sternly orders.

"Your Honor, Judge, I want to ask for your mercy so that I can get help. I don't want to go to jail again. My lawyer here told me that maybe I can get on some kind of program so that I can get some counseling and maybe learn a trade." The man looks up slightly at the Judge with a sad, sincere expression. "I want to change, Judge."

"Mr. Roberts, I am not here to bestow mercy. I am here to uphold my duties and the law." Judge Conner adjusts himself in his seat and leans forward, resting his elbows on the large podium before him and stares intently at the defendant. "So you want another chance, do you? Is that what you are asking for, Mr. Roberts? You would like the court to go easy on you?" he asks, not looking away.

"Yes Sir. I would do my best," the man says in a heavy southern accent, with his head bowed.

"If you were allowed to go into a program, do you truly feel that it would make a difference? Stealing retail goods is a serious offense, Mr. Roberts. The good people of the State of Georgia rely on making a profit to sustain their businesses. If I were to disregard the seriousness of this offense, I do not believe that I would be upholding my job. Do you agree?" the Judge asks.

"I know I did wrong, your Honor, but I needed the tools to try to get work. I know that don't matter in this room. But, I think that I could learn to make different choices, maybe learn to take care of myself and stay out of trouble," the man pleads.

"Mr. Roberts, I will discuss your situation with counsel and perhaps we can find a program *in addition* to your sentence for this crime. I have spent many years in this courtroom and my experience tells me that repeat offenders are not likely to change. Counselor, could you please join me in my chambers during the break so that we may discuss this matter?" the Judge requests.

"Yes your Honor," Sarah answers, giving her client a wink.

Judge Conner signals to the officer in attendance who announces a 20 minute break. Sarah directs Mr. Roberts to take a seat and joins the Judge in his chambers. Judge Conner motions her to sit down as he straightens his robes and eases himself into a large, comfortable leather chair behind a thick, mahogany desk. There is a slight odor of cigar smoke embedded in the paneled walls.

"Make yourself comfortable, Sarah. It's good to see you, as always," he leans back in his chair. "Your career is going quite well. You are a very tenacious, hard working young lady," he compliments.

"Thank you, Judge Conner. Much is thanks to your coaching throughout the years. It meant a lot to me and I am so grateful. Your guidance made a big difference," she responds.

The Judge leans back, pulling a cigar from his desk drawer and runs his fingers down it, raising it to his nose and taking a long sniff. "Sarah, you are an excellent attorney. You've earned a great reputation for yourself in our small town and you've accomplished much for your clients. But, you have always been idealistic and you must know that not everyone can be redeemed. Mr. Roberts for instance, whom I suspect is another pro bono case of yours." The corner of his mouth turns in a half smile. "I am not sure offering assistance is going to change someone who has a history of making bad decisions. It's my duty as you know, to protect the public and uphold the law. Sometimes that means incarceration to drive it home that we won't tolerate breaking the rules. I know that you have faith in these people, but the truth is that they don't change, Sarah. I am not sure a rehab or counseling program is going to make any difference for Mr. Roberts. We are most likely just going to see him in here again, and will have spent valuable taxpayer money on a program that simply bought him time."

"I know," she says contemplating this answer, "but, sending him back to jail . . . that won't help him or the community. He will be there a short period of time and with no options," Sarah pleads.

"Sarah, you are one sweet young lady. How are your parents?" he asks, casually changing the subject.

"Oh," she pauses as she switches her attention. "Well, Dad parks himself in his leather lounger; feet propped up, watching sports on his big screen. Mom is always cooking for whomever my brother drags over to the house. What can I say? They are enjoying life, as always."

"They are good people and I look forward to visiting them this holiday season," the Judge says with a kind smile. "I've thought a lot about your Dad recently. We used to have a lot of fun in law school, your old Dad and I, and he still managed to be at the top of his class. It seemed to come easy for him. He would have been a fabulous attorney. Pity he quit, but he has done well for himself. He has a wonderful family and he has you! I know he's proud of you." He takes a long pause and stares at Sarah. "Sarah, I know that this may be none of my business, but I have always wondered. Is that why you decided to become an attorney? To fulfill his dream and finish what he started?" he asks with a kind, inquisitive face.

Sarah is surprised at his question. "That was a quick transition, Judge Conner! Now why would you ask that out of the blue?"

The Judge looks down at his desk and smiles. "Well, Sarah, I've known you since you were a wee little thing. Always so determined, hardworking, and giving. I've just noticed that you seem to be in this courtroom an awful lot. It's as if you are on a mission and frankly, you don't seem to make time for much else." His face softens.

"Sarah, since I've known you, you've had a soft heart, always helping people and bringing stray and injured animals home." Sarah puts her face in her hands in anticipation of the coming stories. "Didn't you bring a pig home once?" he asks, noting her reaction.

Sarah puts her head on the desk. "The pig story!" she whines quietly then looks up at him. "The baby birds, the dogs, the pig. Yes, I save animals. I saved a pig," she looks as if in extreme pain. "I am sure my parents told you the story." Judge Conner shrugs as if he had not already heard it, prompting her to share it again.

Sarah humors him. "I visited my friend's farm and was shown an adorable new litter of piglets. There was one sweet piglet which was especially small," she pauses as if reliving the moment. "When I found out that he was of no use to the farmer and would be slaughtered or sold off to an experimental lab or something like that, I couldn't bear it. There was no place in this world for the little guy, so I convinced a friend to go back with me late that night to kidnap him." She lowers her voice and begins to giggle.

"We snuck in the barn with nothing but the moonlight to find our way, put him in the back of the car, and sped off. You should have heard him squeal!" She starts to laugh loudly, recalling the details. "Some thanks for rescuing him! He almost blew my cover. Then, of course, I arrived home and had to tell my parents who woke up to squealing. Gosh, does everyone know that story?"

Judge Conner lets out a huge laugh. "I'll pretend I didn't hear the kidnapping part," he says still laughing. "And, yes, everyone does know that story. It's a good one. It's very sweet and I love when you tell it."

Sarah continues. "Well, as you know, it turned out that he wasn't such a runt. He grew up to be quite large!" Sarah reminds him. "We eventually had to retire him to an animal sanctuary."

"He is lucky he didn't retire to the dinner table!" the Judge teases. "Sarah, you are something. You do good things," he says kindly and then becomes serious. "But you can't save everything or everyone, you know."

She looks down at the floor in disappointment, "I know, but I have to try."

Judge Conner nods to himself. "I know that about you, Sarah." He pauses, "Let's see what we can do for your Mr. Roberts. Schedule a date with Claire and we will revisit the case. Just make sure he stays out of trouble until then, or there will be no consideration. I don't want any more tools disappearing from Zack McAllister's hardware store," he warns looking at her over his reading glasses, "And I mean none, Sarah. OK?"

"Thank you, Judge Conner!" Sarah leans forward and gives him a kiss on the cheek.

"Sarah," he pauses, "Don't ever lose your faith. It's refreshing. I don't get to see that very often around here," he holds her hand in a Fatherly way and pats it. Sarah smiles proudly and turns to leave.

"Thank you, Judge Conner." Sarah walks toward the door.

"Oh, and Sarah, send your parents my good wishes and tell them that I look forward to visiting over the holidays!" Judge Conner pulls a lighter out from his top drawer and gets ready to light his cigar.

"I certainly will," she responds. "It will be wonderful to have you join us." She closes the chamber door and smiles to herself, looks at her watch, and gasps. She rushes back to her client where she explains the results of the conversation, escorts him to complete the required paperwork, and quickly bolts to her car.

## Chapter Three
# Jessica Has a Secret

Boutique storefront and restaurant lights randomly pop on and glow as billowing clouds speed past and darkness blankets the town. Sarah holds a clutch purse over her head, trying to protect her mane of hair from a drizzle of rain that floats down and coats the sidewalk. She makes her way to an elegantly carved wooden door flanked by gas lanterns, and enters. It doesn't take long to spot her friend Jessica in the small restaurant who motions to her. Sarah shakes droplets off of her coat and makes her way to the table. The restaurant is narrow with exposed brick walls, and a high ceiling supported by heavy, wooden beams. Happy bartenders tend to chatty customers perched at the copper bar top with a view to an open kitchen where flames randomly shoot from cook tops.

Jessica is a pretty woman in her early 30's with thick auburn hair, large green eyes, and perfect, pale skin. She motions to Sarah to give her a hug, as she takes a sip of her overly full martini glass.

"Hold on there, I'll wait on the hug," Sarah points to the liquid teetering on the edge of the glass, and eases into the chair across from Jessica. "I didn't know we were expecting rain. It's pretty chilly out there, too," Sarah says, shivering.

"We are going into the holiday season, after all. Winter is upon us my friend! Nothing that a good martini can't cure," Jessica smiles and lifts her glass. "By the way, you're late!"

"I know. I'm sorry. Traffic and weather," Sarah responds. "You know how people drive in the south when we get even the slightest rainfall. It's ridiculous."

"Or perhaps it was work," Jessica replies with sarcasm.

Sarah looks down at the table and smiles. "OK, perhaps it *was* work," she admits sheepishly then looks around the room, seeking out a waitress. She spots one and waves for service.

"And?" Jessica asks, tilting her head to one side.

"And what?" Sarah asks.

"How is it going? Have you met any hot Judges or lawyers lately?" Jessica raises her eyebrows.

"Are you kidding?" Sarah frowns. "Why on earth would I want to hang out with someone in law? Even if I did meet someone date worthy, I wouldn't. It would be way too complicated, and not very *professional*," she sarcastically responds.

"Oh yeah, that. Shame," Jessica comments. She places her martini on the table, leans over and sips off the top of it.

"Jessica!" Sarah is embarrassed.

"What? It was too full. I didn't want to spill it," Jessica defends.

"And what about you, Jessica? Anything or any *one* new?" The waitress walks over to the table and Sarah points to Jessica's martini indicating that she will have the same.

"The usual, same old, same old. No prospects. Although there is a hot, young guy in Accounting. I am considering becoming a cougar. I think he'd go for it." She smiles.

"Is it getting that bad?" Sarah asks. "You are barely in your thirties. What is he, 10?"

"Twelve," Jessica says sarcastically. "Sarah, seriously, isn't there anyone you are interested in, remotely? It just seems like you are always working."

"You know there isn't anyone, Jessica. I just don't see the point," Sarah responds in a less than convincing voice.

Jessica stares at her. "Our conversations are getting pretty boring, don't you think? Ms. Wright, what in the heck ever happened to you to make you swear off men?" She becomes very serious. "I'd say it was a heart break, but I happen to know first hand that you've never allowed anyone to get that close to you," she pauses as a waitress places a martini in front of Sarah. "Except that gorgeous guy you dated in school. What was his name? John?" she asks casually.

"John? I never dated John. You know that." Sarah frowns as if insulted at the suggestion.

"Well, it was four years of *something*. Whatever happened to him? He was gorgeous. Why can't I meet someone like that?" Jessica stares dreamily into space.

"That *something* was just studying. And it may have been four years, but it wasn't romantic. Besides, he moved back to New York and I never heard a peep from him. He was always so mysterious about everything and left abruptly. It was odd."

"Really? Maybe he had a deep dark secret. A hidden wife or something and had to cut and run. What was his last name? Verio, Rivero," Jessica continues.

"Don't be silly. And it is Rivera. John Rivera. Why so much interest in John? Where did this come from all of a sudden? I haven't seen him in years." Sarah surveys the menu.

"Rivera! That's right. Latin. Columbian, right? Very handsome guy," Jessica raises an eyebrow. "He has those smoking hot, sexy eyes," she states with a sheepish smile.

"Yes, Columbian, but he was born and raised in New York. His family is from Columbia. And he went back to New York to take a job with a very large law firm bailing out wealthy corporations that poison and kill people," Sarah replies. "That would be the all important reason for his quick exit, I suppose."

"Well. O.K. then," Jessica mocks Sarah's disapproval. "I guess that explains his departure to New York. His desire to defend corporations that kill and mame!" She pauses. "Don't you think that is a bit harsh, especially coming from a fellow attorney? I thought your kind stuck together."

"No, it isn't harsh. It's a fact," Sarah responds, in a confident tone. "Besides having law degrees, our similarities end there."

"Maybe you should tell him in person," Jessica cleverly responds.

"Uh oh," Sarah sits up in her chair. "What is that supposed to mean? What do you know?" She gives Jessica a sly look. "I knew it! There had to be a reason you were bringing this up out of nowhere! Come on, Jessica. *What do you know?*"

Jessica sits back in her chair and sighs. "Oh, just that he is in town." She is pleased to possess such important information.

"Are you serious?" Sarah leans forward and gives her best stern face. "So that is where this was all leading to! Cough it up, girlfriend! Where did you see him and what is he doing here?" Sarah presses. A multitude of feelings flood through Sarah's mind. She adored John. He had been her closest friend and confidante. Sarah liked him much more than she was willing to admit to herself.

Jessica leans forward, anxious to spill her guts. "Well . . . I was shopping at Phillips Mall yesterday and while I was checking out perfumes at the cosmetics counter, I looked up and there he was, looking all tall and handsome."

"Cosmetics?" Sarah's eyes widen.

"Actually, the men's fragrance department. Sarah, the man is gorgeous," Jessica's expression becomes dreamy.

"Jessica, concentrate," Sarah urges.

"O.K., so there I was, putzing around and I see John across from me trying men's fragrances," she continues.

"You are absolutely sure that it was men's? Not women's fragrances?" Sarah pushes for details.

"Yes, darling. Relax. It was men's fragrances. May I continue?" Sarah nods. "So, there I was gawking at him and I realized that I know that face. Of course, it took me a moment since he has been out of the picture for some time, but I realized that it was indeed the same 'John' that you dated."

"Jessica, we didn't date, O.K.? Continue," Sarah prods her.

"Oh, and note that I did check to see if he was wearing a wedding ring," Jessica adds. "There wasn't one, not that you care, right? I mean you being 'just study buddies' and all," she teases and continues. "I realize it is in fact John, but I am not sure if he would remember me. So, I walked over to him and introduced myself."

"And?" Sarah becomes impatient.

"And, he did remember me! Of course only because I reminded him that I was your dearest and closest friend in the world." Jessica smiles with pride and continues. "He certainly perked up when I mentioned your name, Sarah."

"Oh did he?" Sarah tries to appear aloof. "What is he doing here?"

"Well," Jessica continues, "he asked what you were up to, how your practice was going, if you were married, and then he wanted to know if I had your number handy."

"Oh, he asked if I was married did he? And?" Sarah leans forward again.

"I told him you absolutely were not and of course I didn't give him your number!" Jessica says proudly.

"Oh," Sarah seems disappointed then regains her composure. "I mean, of course you didn't. How could you know if I ever wanted to speak with him again," she continues, "especially considering his very rude abrupt departure and then not having the courtesy to stay in touch!"

"Exactly!" Jessica pauses. "Well?"

"Well what?" Sarah is confused.

"I didn't think you would want me handing out your number even though he is totally worth it, Sarah."

"Yes, Jessica, you did mention that he is handsome, that he is smoking hot, bla, bla, bla," Sarah rolls her eyes.

"Do you *want* him to contact you? You don't seem so sure, Sarah. Are you still mad at him?" Jessica leans forward and lowers her voice.

"Sarah, you can't deny that there was an attraction. He was always a really nice guy from what I remember. And smart. You spent years together and you used to be so close. What happened? I mean tell me what *really* happened?"

"You still haven't told me what he is doing here," Sarah continues her inquisition.

Jessica gives Sarah a long stare and continues. "O.K., since you are going to ignore my questions, I shall answer you. He is here to work. Seriously, can you imagine moving to Mayberry from New York?" Jessica teases, taking a large gulp from her glass.

"Easy there, Deputy Fife. Rosedale isn't such a bad place," Sarah defends their small town. "Are you absolutely sure he is *moving* here? *Moving?*"

"Yes! Moving! New York has to be happening in the world of corporate law, don't you think? Not to mention his family is there and it's one heck of an exciting social scene," Jessica responds. "I can't imagine why he would give all of that up to come back here, can you?" The waitress places a basket of bread on the table and pours olive oil into a shallow plate as Sarah stares out the window and contemplates. "So, John Rivera is back in Rosedale. Interesting." She pauses and comes to her senses. "Are you absolutely sure about that?" She looks at Jessica seriously as if questioning a witness.

"Yes! I am sure. He's not here for a case, either, Sarah. He said he joined a firm. Can you imagine? What are the chances? Don't you find that odd?" Jessica tries to get Sarah's response as she blankly stares out the window.

"Yes. I do find that odd," Sarah agrees still deep in thought. "Although, he did intern for a major firm here. I imagine they stayed in touch. He is pretty successful in his field. He's won some pretty big cases."

"So, what are you going to do?" Jessica anxiously asks.

Sarah, still in deep thought looks back at her with a clever smile.

"Absolutely nothing my dear friend. Absolutely nothing." She takes a sip of her martini and leans back in her chair.

"Really? You aren't going to try to contact him?"

"I certainly will not! After all of these years? No way. I guess he has a reason for abandoning our relationship, so we'll just leave it at that," Sarah looks at Jessica with a matter-of-fact expression.

"You *are* mad at him! I think that you had feelings for him whether you admit it or not. Suit yourself," Jessica frowns.

"May we talk about something else? I'd like to hear about you and not spend our time talking about John Rivera."

"OK, girlfriend," Jessica responds, "I think you two had something going on. It's never too late!" Jessica is obviously having fun with the conversation.

"Thank you. I appreciate your advice," Sarah smirks. "Now may we change the subject? There are more interesting things to discuss, like my parents' upcoming Christmas party."

"Oh! I can't wait to go to your parents' place for Christmas! We always have such a good time," Jessica squeals in delight.

"In fact, I'll be over there decorating the tree this weekend," Sarah is relieved to divert Jessica's attention.

"Oh fun!" Jessica takes the final sip of her martini.

A waitress walks around the restaurant, lighting candles on tables as the friends continue to share stories and laugh.

## Chapter Four

# A Visit with the Fam

It is dusk as Sarah turns on to her parents' street and is greeted with twinkling Christmas lights on many of the neighbor's homes. She parks in their driveway and climbs out of her older, BMW when she hears a small voice.

"Sarah! Hello there!" yells a hunched over, white haired lady from the home next door. "How is our successful lawyer? We miss you!" The elderly woman tightly clutches a walker, navigating her way down her driveway toward her mailbox.

"Mrs. Costello, it's wonderful to see you! Let me help you. It's slick out here," Sarah quickly runs to the mailbox and retrieves the contents. She joins the tiny woman, giving her a gentle hug and kiss on the cheek. "I miss you too! You shouldn't be out alone in the dark like this," Sarah places her arm around Mrs. Costello's shoulders and slowly walks the fragile woman back to the porch steps. "How have you been?" Sarah politely asks.

"Sarah, it's so good to see you! I am just the same as always, hobbling around as you can see. I sit in my favorite chair at my window and watch the world go by," she smiles.

"I see that the neighbors are getting in the spirit," Sarah comments as she examines the colorful Christmas lights and lawn decorations.

"Well, you know this one has been preparing to put up the crazy tree," Mrs. Costello points across the street at the same home that Sarah dreamt about earlier, now dark and run down.

"Oh, right, the Landis house. I just had a funny dream about that, when we were kids and Mrs. Landis used to get angry with us. Not sure why that was on my mind."

"Probably because Christmas is upon us and you know Mr. Landis will be up to his strange behavior. In fact, he was preparing all day to put that flashy Christmas tree up," Mrs. Costello shakes her head.

Sarah stares at the home. "I guess it wouldn't be Christmas unless Mr. Landis put his tree on his roof. Ever since I was a kid, I remember the fights, his wife always yelling, and then silence for so many years. But, Mr. Landis always seemed like such a nice man. Do you ever see any family or friends over there?" Sarah asks.

"No. It's been at least fifteen years, Sarah. Nothing has changed. Mr. Landis is still over there, by himself. The house is disintegrating around him. But that tree," she shakes her head. "Every year, that crazy, lit tree goes up on that roof. It seems to be the only thing that he looks forward to." Mrs. Costello looks intently at Sarah. "I try not to be nosey, but it's hard not to see what goes on when you sit at the window all day. Every street has the old, nosey neighbor!" she laughs loudly. "There isn't much that I miss. I hardly ever see him leave except on his bike to get groceries once in a while. If it weren't for that and the annual tree display, I'd wonder if he was alive!"

"Well, I am here to help my parents put up their tree, early as usual. You know how they love Christmas. Mrs. Costello, I hope that you will be joining us again for the holidays," Sarah beckons.

"You are so kind. It's been so long since my Henry passed, but it never stops being lonely during the holidays. You know I always look forward to spending Christmas with all of you." She begins to step into her entry way and pauses. "I see that you haven't brought any young men home to meet your parents, Sarah."

"I guess you *don't* miss anything!" Sarah wrinkles her nose and smiles. "Truth is I don't really have time for that, Mrs. Costello. I am pretty busy with work. No time for boys!" She holds the old lady's arm to steady her as she steps into her house.

"Oh, I'm sure, my dear. I'm sure. Now don't let me hold you up.

You get in that house to decorate that tree and visit with your parents," she demands. "Please send my good wishes."

"I will Mrs. Costello, and I look forward to catching up with you at our Christmas party." Sarah walks back to her parents' home and pauses on their porch where a wreath hangs. She looks back at the dark house across the street remembering when Mr. Landis would be seen pushing his son down the street in a stroller after a heated argument with his wife.

"Are you coming inside, or are you going to enjoy the crisp evening air?" Sarah's father stands at the door, now open.

"Oh Dad! Sorry. I was just day dreaming." She turns and gives him a big hug.

"Day dreaming on the porch? Get your toosh in here! We have food, we have a tree, and I have one heck of a fire going in the fireplace!"

The Wright home is filled with smells of southern cooking and smoking logs that burn brightly in the hearth. Christmas music is playing. Sarah removes her coat and makes her way to the kitchen where her brother and Mother are loudly talking and preparing food. They cheer as she enters the room.

"Hey! There she is!" her Mother gives her a big hug and kiss. Her kind face shows smile lines and her green eyes, like her daughter's, shine brightly. "Ohhhh, I miss this," she says hugging her tighter.

"Mom, really. I'm 33 years old!" Sarah reminds her. "Exactly what do you miss?"

"This," Mom says still holding her, "hugging you whenever I want to." She wipes a tear from her eye.

"Mom, I live three miles from here. It's a small town. What's gotten into you?" Sarah says laughing and hugging her back.

"I know, I know," she replies. "The holidays are almost here and I always get a little sentimental. Between you and your brother whom we hardly get to see, I'm feeling a bit lonely. He has a new girlfriend, you know."

"Doug? Yes, so I have heard," Sarah replies, examining the array of food her Mother has prepared.

"Are you two talking about me?" Doug yells from the dining room as he places a stack of plates on the table.

"Yes, and this is a private conversation!" Sarah yells back as she pulls a drinking glass from a cupboard.

"Well, if it concerns me and Stephanie it is certainly my business," he replies.

"So, Mom, aren't we trimming the tree a bit early this year?" Sarah grabs a carrot from a plate and dips it in a bowl of hummus. She steps through the doorway to view the stack of boxes packed with shiny bulbs surrounding the bare tree.

"Oh, you know your Mother," Sarah's Father replies as he enters the kitchen and begins to pull out silverware. "She loves Christmas and the tradition and whole hoopla around it."

"Speaking of traditions, I was just talking to Mrs. Costello about our enthusiastic neighbor and *his* tradition," Sarah says.

"Oh, Mr. Landis. Yep, he is getting ready to put his tree up. We rarely see him until he is tinkering on that roof once a year or when the law enforcement visits."

"Geez, are they still hauling him in for that?" Sarah asks.

"You should know, Sarah. You're at that courthouse 24/7," her Father comments.

"Dear Mrs. Costello. We must have her over for the holidays," her Mother responds.

"I invited her, Mom. She pretty much knows that she is a permanent guest every holiday," Sarah reminds her.

Sarah walks into the living room and peers out the window across the street. A bright moon lights up the roof tops and Sarah can see that Mr. Landis has a long ladder which he steadily sets up against his house. He carefully climbs to the top, pulling a rope along with him. As he reaches the roof, he steadies himself and wraps the rope around the chimney, dropping the other end to the ground. He slowly climbs back down the ladder where he fastens the end to a Christmas tree which is lying on the ground and pulls the tree up with his crude wench system. A yank at a time, it finally reaches the roof where he secures the rope. Climbing back up the ladder, he unties the tree and hauls it to a center spot of the roof where he awkwardly hammers it onto a wooden pole. It is noticeably cocked to one side. A couple on an evening stroll point at the messy display and shake their heads in disapproval.

"If you are looking for the lighter for the candles, it's in the pantry," Sarah's Mother directs her Father as she sees him searching through drawers.

"I *have* seen him in the courtroom a few times around the holidays. A couple of years ago I offered my services, pro bono. He didn't want help," Sarah adds.

"I don't understand," her Mother stops and looks at Sarah. "Exactly why does he end up in a courtroom every year? Besides creating some real excitement for this neighborhood, I am not quite sure I understand what a Christmas tree on the roof has to do with the law. I admit it is a bit distasteful, but it doesn't harm anyone."

"It's a major building code violation, Mom," Sarah explains. "A big fire hazard, more than anything. It is dangerous because of how it's attached, and it's not in compliance. He needs to get a permit, which I am sure would never be issued. And he needs to make sure that tree doesn't go up in flames. With all of those cords hanging down, I am surprised it hasn't after all of these years." She pauses. "I think he is emotionally disturbed."

Mr. Landis continues to work on decorating his tree, climbing up and down the ladder with as many strings of lights as he can carry. He pays no attention to where he places them, throwing them on in massive, uneven clumps. Numerous extension cords hang from the roof. He continues to load the tree until the branches are heavy and barely holding up against the weight.

"Well, I think we have all figured out that he is disturbed. But, I look forward to the display. It's a tradition around here," Sarah's Dad adds as he finds matches and proceeds to light candles on the dining room table.

"I think Sarah is right. He has a screw loose!" her brother adds.

"Doug!" her Mother exclaims. "If putting a tree on the roof is the worst thing he does then I am fine with that." Her Mom pulls out steaming lasagna and begins to cut it up. "Sarah, speaking of the courthouse, how is everything going for you?"

"Oh yeah, that reminds me! Judge Conner sends his regards and will be visiting over the holidays." Sarah takes a seat at the table.

"Oh how wonderful!" her Mother says.

"Geez, I haven't seen Joe Conner in a while. How is he doing?" Dad asks.

"Great. Hasn't changed a bit. Just as tough and sweet as ever," Sarah pauses. "You know, he recently asked me an odd question."

"What is an odd question?" Dad asks.

"Well, we were going over a case and he wanted to know if I had become a defense attorney because of you." Sarah looks at her Father.

"Me?" her Father looks surprised. "You mean because I dropped out of law school?"

"I guess so," Sarah responds. "I had to admit that he got me thinking." She examines her Father's face.

"Sarah, you aren't feeling any strange guilt thing because I dropped out to support my family are you?" he continues.

"No, of course not," she begins to fiddle with her hands.

"Sarah, I didn't need you to become an attorney to fulfill my dreams, if that is what you mean. I could have done that myself. Maybe working in construction isn't the epitome of success, but I have no regrets." He looks closely at her, "None."

Mom places more food on the table. "So, where is this coming from, kiddo? Why bring this up now?" she asks.

"Sarah? Where is this coming from?" her Dad asks.

"I don't know. I guess when Judge Conner asked me, he must have thought that something was there. I mean, he knew Dad so well in law school and all."

"Well, if there is any 'unfinished business' idea in your head regarding your father's career, remove it. Your Dad and I are happy. But, I can't speak for why you are so determined with your career and afraid to commit to a man, or even dating for that matter," her Mom peers at her intently. "I hope it isn't because you are afraid that you will end up like your dear Ma and Pa, is it? God forbid you fall in love and worse, have a child and stop working those insane hours!"

"Mother! No! That isn't what I was getting at!" Sarah shouts. "But, I have to admit that between Judge Conner's comment and Jessica questioning my love life, maybe there is something there I need to look at closer."

"Oh, how is Jessica? You know your friends sometimes know you better than you know yourself. You may want to give it some consideration, Sarah. You have been totally focused on your work and you don't seem to be taking any time out for much other than those dog rescues of yours," her Father comments.

"Now, everyone, please eat while the food is still hot," her Mother orders.

Doug is busy piling food on his plate, unaffected by the serious discussion. He pauses and stares at his sister. "So, Sarah *are* you dating anyone?"

"Thanks, Doug," Sarah gives her brother a serious stare.

"Hey, don't blame me! You guys brought it up and you're the 33 year old, soon to be 34 year old, single woman who, by the way, doesn't seem to have any prospects," he adds.

Sarah rolls her eyes, "Uh oh, I can see where this is going. I truly appreciate your concern, Doug."

"Well, Sarah, now that the subject has come up, you haven't so much as brought one man home to meet us," Dad points out as he carves out a piece of lasagna.

"Sarah, don't listen to your Father. If you want to remain single your entire life, we support your decision," Mom smiles.

"Yeah, Sarah. If you want to be an old maid, we totally support that! I will have a permanent babysitter when I have a family," Doug laughs and takes another bite of food.

"Oh boy," Sarah throws her arms up. "O.K., everyone, enough about my dating life. Believe me, I am well aware that it is glaringly non-existent as everyone reminds me."

"So, Doug, we have our big holiday celebration coming up. Will you be bringing your beloved?" Dad asks.

"Are we having the usual gathering?" Doug continues to eat at a steady pace.

"Doug, you know better than to ask that question. Your Father is already perfecting his rum eggnog recipe!" Mom raises her eyebrows as she looks at Dad.

"Then count Stephanie and me in. It's never boring with Dad's home made rum eggnog! Mrs. Costello *loves* it. Remember last year when I had to walk her back home? *She* was all happy. That was one wobbly walker trip back,'" Doug smiles, pleased that he earned a big round of laughter from the family.

"Yes, we certainly have some fun memories of those holiday parties. I will be bringing Jessica if that's O.K." Sarah interrupts.

"Jessica is always welcome. You know that," her Mother assures her, grabbing Sarah's hand. "You know we love you kids no matter what, don't you?"

"You mean even if Sarah ends up being an old maid?" Doug teases once again.

"May we change the subject? There is a tree waiting to be decorated," Sarah walks over to a box of ornaments and begins to pick out a few that she carefully places on the tree.

"Sarah is right," Dad smiles and puts his plate down, walks to his wife, giving her a solid hug and kiss on the lips. "It's the holiday season and we must be of good cheer!"

Doug raises a wine glass. "Here! Here!"

Sarah grabs her glass and clinks Doug's. She looks around the cozy room, looks back at Doug, her hugging parents, then takes a big gulp. "Bottom's up!"

## Chapter Five

# An Awkward Reunion

As Sarah starts up the courthouse steps, she sees that the massive fir tree on the lawn is now loaded with multi-colored lights and shiny bulbs. The weight of the decorations does not phase the mighty tree which stands steadfast in proud display. Sarah pauses to admire its awesome beauty. She pulls her coat tightly around her body as a cold wind sweeps up the steps and swirls about her prompting her to seek warmth in the confines of the building.

"Hi Claire," Sarah steps up to the check-in counter where she is greeted by the rosy cheeked clerk.

"Hello Miss Wright. Are you ready for the holidays?" she asks sorting through files.

"Oh, as ready as ever," Sarah responds. "My parents already have their tree up and decorated."

"And what about your tree? Here you go," she pushes a stack of papers toward her, as Sarah is signing in.

"Oh, I'm working on it," she winks.

"Courtroom A, Sarah," Claire points.

Sarah turns and walks down the hall to the last door where she sees her client sitting on a bench just outside. They shake hands and enter the courtroom, taking a seat toward the back, and silently wait for their case to begin. A defense attorney at the front of the room begins to speak, gesturing to the other side of the courtroom where the plaintiff, a middle aged man in a wheel chair, sits listening intently.

"Your Honor, I was not informed of the new evidence the prosecution is about to present today. I will need time to properly review the documentation. Although my client, Somadine Pharmaceuticals, is certainly sensitive to the condition of the plaintiff and urgency of this matter, in order to properly prepare my case, additional time will be required."

"Counselor Hutchins," Judge Conner turns to the grey haired plaintiff's attorney, "as you know the defense must have time to review the new evidence which should have been made available, might I remind you."

"Of course your Honor. This was not intentional," the attorney responds. "They are new developments discovered prior to presenting today and we were unable to share them in time."

"Counselor Rivera, will two weeks be sufficient?" Judge Conner asks the young defense attorney.

Sarah abruptly sits up. "Rivera?" she whispers to herself out loud, directing her attention away from her paperwork and to the front of the courtroom. There stands a tall, handsome man with broad shoulders dressed in an impeccable suit.

"Yes your Honor. Thank you," the handsome attorney responds.

"Counselor," Judge Conner addresses the plaintiff's attorney, acknowledging the man seated in a wheelchair beside him, "I hope that this does not inconvenience your client. Please visit the front desk and reschedule." The Judge hands him a signed document.

"Due to the holiday season coming upon us, we shall revisit this case after Christmas. Counselor Rivera, that should give you more than enough time."

"Thank you, your Honor. It does." The attorney nods to the Judge and walks back to his briefcase where he begins to pack up. He glances around the courtroom and catches the sight of Sarah, noticeably perks up, and gives her a big smile. Sarah returns the smile, her lip twitching nervously as she realizes that it is indeed John Rivera. He quickly fastens his briefcase and walks toward her.

As he reaches Sarah's bench, he leans close to her ear, keeping his voice down. "Ms. Wright, I didn't expect to see your beautiful face. What a pleasant surprise."

"It certainly has been a long time," Sarah adjusts her blouse as she feels her chest and neck flush. Red blotches quickly spread to her cheeks and ears. "I thought you were lighting the Big Apple on fire," she responds.

"I guess I am just a small town boy at heart." He pauses and leans in closely. "I received an offer from a firm here in town that I couldn't turn down. It must be destiny, don't you think?" he smiles sweetly.

"Oh, is that what you call it? Interesting," she purses her lips and nods.

John kneels down closer so as not to disturb the proceedings, and lowers his voice. "Still saving the world I see," he motions to the man sitting next to her, careful that her client does not hear.

"Still defending the pharmaceutical industry against its human experiments?" Sarah fires back.

"Don't forget defending those asbestos and lead based paint companies that I've added to my repertoire," he responds still smiling. Sarah squints at him.

"Do they throw in free prescriptions to help you sleep at night?" Sarah is pleased with her witty response.

"It's nice to know that you haven't lost that feisty personality and quirky sense of humor that I always loved," John adds. Sarah gives a mock, sweet smile.

"Ms. Wright!" Judge Conner shouts, "May we begin?" he says peering over a paper he holds in front of his face. "That is, if you are done flirting."

Embarrassed, Sarah responds. Her red blotches spread further up her face. "Yes, of course your Honor. My apologies." She nervously clears her voice.

"Then step forward and proceed," Judge Conner says, pointing to the space in front of his bench.

Sarah walks to the head of the courtroom as John laughs under his breath and retreats to the hallway.

Judge Conner leans over, careful to keep his voice down. "Now that Mr. Rivera is in town, you may want to consider taking a little time out for a date, Sarah. Perhaps you two can make good on unfinished business from law school."

Sarah stutters, "Your, your Honor. I, I . . ."

The Judge sits up and speaks loudly, "Counselor Wright, I see that your client, Mr. Adkins, has met all of the court requirements. I think that we can save some time here. I am suspending jail time and placing Mr. Adkins on probation. Please escort your client to our front desk where we will set up a schedule for him that includes working with a probation officer. Please note the additional requirements placed on Mr. Adkins which the officer will monitor." The Judge looks squarely at Mr. Adkins. "I expect good things from you. Your attorney has jumped through many hoops to assure that you received another chance at contributing to our community in a positive way, not to mention yourself. I hope that you appreciate those efforts."

The man perks up and produces a large, toothless smile. He nods his head in enthusiasm as though a light has been turned on inside of him.

"We may proceed with the next case. Thank you Counselor Wright," the Judge leans forward and crooks his finger, luring her to approach the bench. "I think that things are about to get interesting around the holidays." He winks.

"Judge Conner!" Sarah awkwardly responds. She turns and gestures to her client to follow her.

"Thank you, Ms. Wright," Mr. Adkins says to Sarah as he tries to keep up with her. "Much appreciated."

"Larry, you are very welcome, and please call me Sarah," she responds once outside the courtroom. "Now, go check in. Your paperwork will come out shortly and you'll be meeting with a probation officer who will go over all of the requirements. I'll check back with you before you leave." The man nods and heads down the hallway.

As Sarah gains her composure, she sees John speaking to another attorney nearby. She quickly heads in the opposite direction when John spots her, his face lighting up. He excuses himself from the conversation and picks up his pace.

"Hey, Sarah, wait up! Sarah! How did it go in there?" he calls out.

Sarah stops, realizing that there is no way to avoid interaction. "Fine, thanks. We are just finishing up some paperwork."

John approaches her. "Great, then you have time to grab a coffee and catch up." Sarah looks reluctant. "Come on! You just said you have to wait on your client. Besides, I'm buying," he beckons and looks closely into her eyes. "I don't bite Sarah."

"I know," she says noticeably flustered, trying to laugh and act casual. "Sure, let's go have a coffee," she smiles.

Her thoughts go back to the two of them at the law library, studying, laughing and sharing every waking hour together. John was her rock and her best friend -- the person whom she looked up to and counted on most. He was also the same person who mysteriously left her, without explanation. There he casually stood, as if he had just come back from a vacation.

John leads them down the hall with Sarah closely behind. "Well, come on slow poke," he says grabbing her arm and pulling her with him.

"Wait," Sarah stops, places her hands on his shoulders and turns him around, looking him squarely in the face. "Stop for just a minute, John. I'm sorry, but this is all a bit weird. You show up here after all of these years and ask me to have coffee like it's just any day."

John looks at her as if he doesn't know what she is talking about and gives a sheepish grin.

"John! There is nothing funny about this. Seriously, it was shocking to see you standing in the courthouse, in my tiny little southern town without any warning. You've been gone for years! With not so much as a postcard, I might add." Sarah studies him closely and sees that he has matured, looking even more handsome than she had remembered. She continues, "Then out of the blue, you move from New York to Rosedale? If Jessica hadn't told me that you were back in town, I would be even more astounded. Could you possibly have gotten such a great offer that you would leave New York? This makes no sense to me."

John stares at her with his mouth slightly open, "Oh, so Jessica *did* tell you that I was back. I figured that the news would travel quickly. O.K. my dear girl, let's slow down." He takes her hand. "Must we have this discussion right now in the hallway? Let's go have that coffee, and take it one step at a time," he responds with a kind and reassuring look. "Yes?"

Sarah looks at him intently, blinks, and sighs, "O.K., sure."

They walk to the courthouse coffee shop where they join a short line of people. Both grab disposable cups and fill them with steaming coffee from large, silver tanks.

"So, let's start with *why* I am here." John loads up his coffee with cream and sugar. "As you know, I interned with a local firm for a period of time."

"Yes, I remember." Sarah responds, rifling through a basket to find a brown sugar packet.

"Well, when I left to work in New York, they stayed in touch with me. They were aware of a few cases that I landed and after a few years recruited me. I guess that they wanted to bring a bit of 'big city' to this small town. To get to the point, they made me an incredible offer and I took it." John stops and looks at Sarah who has a look of disbelief. "What? What is that look? I've always liked it here. New York was getting old for me."

"Oh really? I find that hard to believe," she continues. "Just like that, you dump the glamour life and job and pop back to the town that, might I remind you, you couldn't wait to get out of."

"I could elaborate, but what's the point? I'm here now, right?" John gives her a big smile.

"Well, it's a surprise," she responds, fidgeting.

"Yes, so I am beginning to see," John says.

"Might I say that I think you are being modest, John. You landed more than just a few big cases since you left Rosedale," she begins to walk through the line to the cash register. "Your firm secured a super star. That is a big accomplishment for a Rosedale practice. Almost unheard of, actually."

"Hey, hey, now don't make fun of our special town here which, might I add, is your birth place. That alone makes it a pretty special place," he teases. They arrive at the cash register where John pays for their coffees.

"Perhaps, but New York it isn't," Sarah adds.

"To tell the truth," John stops and waits until they walk away from the cash register to a small table in the corner. "New York *was* great. New York will always be great. But I loved living here. There is a lot that I missed." He gives Sarah a direct stare, making her uncomfortable.

"Oh, well, yes," she stutters a bit as she situates herself in a plastic chair. "It certainly is a nice, friendly little town," she begins to compose herself and gives him a long stare.

"Seriously John, you can't tell me that you have missed Doc Patton's rooster crowing over beeping taxis, or Miss Adelson's experimental pot pies over five star restaurants, or our annual Christmas tree lighting ceremony over the Macy's Day Parade?"

"The Pot Hole is still going? Miss Adelson is still making those crazy pot pies? Geez, I have to get over there and try a few!" He laughs and then looks at Sarah with a serious face. "Sarah. Dear sweet Sarah, how do you like saving the world? Are you happy with your chosen career path?" John changes the subject.

"Oh, I guess it's like anything else. I have my good days and my bad," she responds, blowing on her hot coffee.

"Seriously, Sarah. Are you happy?" John asks sincerely.

Sarah looks off into the distance and thinks. "If my efforts cause one person to make a positive change in their life, I feel pretty good about that." She looks at John directly. "I guess I just have faith that somehow I can make a difference. We don't always have to understand people and their behavior. We just need to be there for them. That may sound corny to you, especially coming from an attorney." She looks at him and sees a look of confusion. "Don't you have faith in anything, John? I mean just know that you must do what feels right, even if you don't know why?" she asks.

"I have faith in my clients paying their bills," he teases.

"Classic," Sarah replies, "Spoken like a true attorney. John, it can't always be about money."

"Well," John continues, "I collect the facts and I build my case. You have clients that steal and you hope you can change them. I see someone who just steals or does some other stupid act. Faith isn't a factor. Good is good and bad is bad. What we do is a job. Right or wrong, crooks or victims, getting our clients off the hook is what we do, what we get paid for," he answers.

"I am sorry that you see it that way," Sarah responds looking disappointed, "because the possibilities are endless. Despite the less-than-attractive reputation attorneys have, it is possible to bring good into our profession."

"Oh, so you are looking to upgrade the lowly status of trial lawyers?" John laughs out loud. "Well, that is noble, Sarah, but we are what we are and I am O.K. with that. We're a different breed. If there weren't people willing to compromise their own morals, then who would defend the bad guys? We keep a lot of people employed. Think of all of the jobs lost if we didn't come to the rescue of the evil and the damned!"

Sarah laughs, reaches across the table and teasingly gives his arm a light punch.

"Ouch! You still pack a punch!" he dramatically feigns pain.

"Well, John, how about yourself? You were always a super star in law school, top of the class, driven, corporate law all the way. Is it all that *you* thought it'd be? Besides making the big dollars, that is," she teases.

"I don't always like the circumstances of the case. But, I do my job and I do it well. I try not to get hung up on the moral details. I simply carry out the wishes of my client," John responds.

"I suppose you are right. It's a job and you certainly are good at it from what I've heard," Sarah tries not to show her disapproval. "You were always determined, that's for sure. I've heard about some major cases that you have won, so congratulations on that," she comments struggling to show enthusiasm.

"Ahhh, I sense disapproval!" John comments.

"Well," she hesitates, "I just think our lives . . . our careers, have to be about more than financial gain. I mean, you can have both you know. Let's face it. Your clients have deep pockets. They have a huge advantage and no conscience."

"Hmmm, you do have a point there," John blows on his coffee and takes a sip, "especially about the deep pockets." He cocks his head slightly to one side and looks at her inquisitively. "So, Sarah, I know that you and I are on opposite sides of the defense corners. But, let's talk about something more interesting. Is there a Mr. Sarah?"

"John, I think you know me well enough. I love this," she looks around the room. "It's what I live for." She takes another sip of coffee. John raises his eyebrows, waiting for an answer. She realizes she can't avoid giving him one. "No, there is no one. I have been pretty much dedicated to my work."

"And your animals from what I remember. You know, Sarah, you can have your career, your charitable work, *and* have love in your life. Besides, you are Super Woman. If anyone can handle all of it and do it well, it would be you. I have to say that some poor schmuck is missing out on something incredible." Sarah looks up, surprised at his comment. John continues, "Is that why you would never go out with me? I am the evil, corporate attorney with no conscience? The kind of guy you couldn't imagine spending time with?"

"No!" Sarah says acting surprised at the question. "I was always very busy. We were always studying and focused on school and getting our careers going. Then you moved to New York to practice." She pauses. "Very quickly, I might add."

"Yes, I did move to New York, but now I'm back! Just think of all of the catching up we can do! No more long nights studying, weekends at the law library or stressing over exams. Now we can just stress out over our work and commiserate. Perhaps we can find the time?" He gives her a flirtatious stare. He is silent for a moment then becomes serious. "Sarah, I know I left abruptly, and I know that we lost touch. But, I *am* back and I feel that there was an opportunity missed." Sarah looks doubtful. "I mean it. You can't tell me that you never thought that. I mean, I know that we were good friends and everything, but I feel like there is unfinished business."

"I guess you could say that. John, you left without a 'good bye' and no contact after that whatsoever. What do you want me to say?" Sarah looks down at the table surface and stares, avoiding eye contact. "It's been years. How do you explain that? And now you want to catch up? You are one strange guy." She suddenly looks at her watch, "Wow, it's time that I get back to my client." She quickly stands. "Thanks for the coffee."

As she turns to walk away, John stands and touches her shoulder. "Sarah, it would be really nice if we could go out to dinner one night, just the two of us. May I call you?"

"John," she pauses and smiles. "That is a nice offer. It really is and I appreciate it." She stops, decides not to say what she really thinks, and continues. "Again, thanks for the coffee, and the *interesting* conversation," she smiles. "It is really great to see you again." She picks up her coffee and begins to walk away.

"Hey!" John calls out. "You didn't answer me. How about taking some time to go out with your old law school buddy?"

"Sure," Sarah says without looking back. "I'll get back to you." She waves her hand in the air.

"But you don't have my number! Sarah? Sarah!" John shouts as she disappears around a corner. John finds himself standing alone. He slowly shakes his head, "She won't call."

## Chapter Six
# Who Is Mr. Landis?

S arah picks up her pace as she takes on a gentle, rolling hill that leads out of her neighborhood. She waves to the occasional neighbor and shopkeeper, keeping a steady pace as she dodges dog walkers and pedestrians. Sarah's pony tail swings back and forth, as she slows down, eventually stopping to catch her breath and stretch her leg muscles.

"Hey Sarah," a young man yells from a building doorway. "We have three tenants anxiously waiting for you!"

"Are they ready?" Sarah walks to the building and enters a small reception area. The young man follows her.

"Sure are! Hold tight." He walks through a door and disappears. An attractive auburn haired woman greets Sarah at the reception counter.

"Hello there, Sarah. How are things?"

"Great, Ellen. I'll be keeping the crew over the holidays, so I will just bring them home with me today after our walk if that is O.K.," Sarah smiles as she eyes a cheap, fake tree that stands, glittering in the corner of the reception area.

"Wonderful. They are all yours, Sarah. We really appreciate it. It's tough to get walkers over the holidays," Ellen looks to the door as a tiny, old, crumpled woman enters and slowly shuffles to the large jar of dog treats sitting on the counter.

"Hi Bell," Ellen greets the woman. "Here for Emma's daily treat?"

The woman quietly reaches into the jar, ignoring the receptionist, removes several dog treats and slowly shuffles back out the door. Outside stands an obese Terrier with a white whiskered face, patiently waiting and wagging its stubby tail.

"Still coming in here, is she?" Sarah stares at the woman who barely weighing 100 pounds, bends over and carefully feeds the grateful animal.

"Oh yes. Bell takes care of that dog of hers above all else. I have no idea how that woman stays alive. She is so thin and I worry about her, with winter coming on."

"I know," Sarah shakes her head, still staring at the woman. "There are a few sad souls in this town with stories we'll never know or understand. I hear that she has money. Comes from a wealthy family, but still wanders the streets. It is a mystery."

"That it is," Ellen agrees. "Oh, here come the kids!"

The young man reappears with three mutts who begin to bark and pull on their leashes at the sight of Sarah.

"Well, look at these happy faces!" She leans over and hugs them all as tails wag and they jump on her, licking her face in excitement.

"Have a good walk and a wonderful holiday! Wear them out, Sarah. They've been bouncing off the walls with our reduced Christmas staff. Thanks for giving three pups a happy Christmas."

"No problem, Ellen. I'll bring back three tuckered pups after the holidays." Sarah is yanked out the door as the young man opens it and the dogs leap to freedom. The dogs bark and tug at their leashes as they launch into a full sprint.

"OK, kids, slow down!" Sarah runs faster to keep up with them as they drag her down the sidewalk.

"Hey Sarah!" a neighbor across the street waves, laughing at the frantic sight as he shuffles to his car with packages.

"Hello Mr. Evans!" Sarah shouts back as she is pulled down the street. Several other passersby wave and yell greetings, laughing at the chaotic sight.

Sarah continues several blocks before the dogs begin to settle down and trot at a reasonable pace. Sarah realizes that she is close to her parents' home. As she catches her breath, she sees a police car in a driveway several homes in the distance. A police officer is walking back to his squad car as she comes upon the house.

"Hey, Ted," Sarah greets the officer as she sees that he is parked at the Landis house. The flashy, side cocked tree perched on the roof landmarks the otherwise forgettable and dilapidated property.

"Is everything OK? Is it Mr. Landis's tree again?" Sarah asks.

"Yes, Ma'am. Mr. Landis and I are old friends, I'm afraid," he gives a weak smile.

"I know," Sarah shakes her head. "I wish that there was something we . . . I could do."

"Nothing that anyone can do until he takes that tree down. That isn't going to happen any time soon," the officer answers. "I wish that I didn't have to make this trip, but I am afraid he is going back into the courtroom," he shakes his head and looks up at the dazzling, lopsided tree, lights flashing even in the daylight hours.

"You have to do your job, Ted," Sarah consoles him.

"I know, but it doesn't feel right," he responds sadly looking back at the house. "Not at Christmas time. He doesn't seem to have anything else to look forward to, you know?"

"Yes, I know. But, you really don't have a choice, Ted," she responds.

"Well, you have a good day, Miss Sarah," Ted tips his officer's hat.

"Thank you, Ted. You too," Sarah continues to walk her furry friends down the street. She takes a turn at the end of the block, heading to the courthouse. As she reaches the walkway in front of the building, she hears a voice from behind.

"You just can't stay away from this place can you? Not even on your day off," Judge Conner smiles, as Sarah turns to see him standing only a few feet away.

"Caught me," she laughs.

"Who are your friends here?" The Judge bends down and gives each dog a big pat on the head, tails wagging, each giving an occasional jump.

"Oh, my orphan buddies. I walk them and occasionally foster them until we can get them into good homes." She points at each, "This is Bo, Sugar here, and the little guy is Doogie." The dogs seem to understand Sarah, wagging and giving what appear to be smiles. "Actually, I was out for a run and wanted to stop by to look into something."

"You never stop working, Sarah. What is it this time?" The Judge shakes his head.

"It's Mr. Landis, my parent's neighbor. You know, the guy who puts the Christmas tree on his roof," she reminds him.

"Oh, I am well aware of Mr. Landis. I can't tell you 'why,' but I can certainly tell you 'what.' It is an ongoing issue. Why are you asking about Mr. Landis after all of these years?" he asks.

"Well, I was jogging past my parents' house and I saw the police over there, again. It just seems so sad. Even Ted hates having to go over there. I was wondering if I could look at his files. I don't know. I just thought that maybe there was something there." She looks sincerely at the Judge.

"I sense another pro bono case coming. In my opinion, he seems of sound of mind, which translates to 'he is harmless.' After that, I am not sure what to think. Obviously there are some issues that none of us seem to have insight into. My advice, Sarah is that you just leave it be. Mr. Landis has never sought help nor accepted it. I don't think that there is anything new that you will discover that will change a thing," the Judge advises.

Sarah gives Judge Conner a sad face and stares at him. "Oh, Sarah. Is it that important to you?" he beckons. She looks at him with a slight smile. "O.K. then, young lady. You can go ahead and look at his files, but don't hold out any hope. I think he likes coming in here every year. Perhaps he likes the attention. No one knows. Don't expect to accomplish anything." Judge Conner pauses and looks at her thoughtfully. "Why don't you stay here with the pooches and I'll go get your files. Be sure to bring them back by tomorrow. The files, not the pooches. We'll be needing them shortly." Sarah giggles. "Don't worry. I will see to it that Mr. Landis has a nice, hot meal at Christmas in his jail cell. Now come on, you sit here with your friends and I'll fetch them for you."

"Thank you, Judge Conner." Sarah is pleased. The Judge nods his head, turns and disappears into the courthouse.

"You're welcome, Sarah." The Judge slowly plods up the steps and into the building, shaking his head. "That girl," he laughs.

"Hey there, Claire!" Judge Conner leans over the counter, his big frame taking up most of it. "Can you dig out the Landis files for me?"

Claire peers up from her reading glasses, "Of course, Judge Conner. Is our dear Mr. Landis here for the roof top Christmas tree violation so soon?"

"Not yet. Actually, Counselor Wright requested the files and I am humoring her." The Judge gives Claire a reassuring smile.

"Oh no, not another charity case of hers," Claire frowns. "She hardly has time for her paid clients and animal rescues."

"Funny you mention that. She happens to be outside with a crew of her furry friends. I thought I'd oblige her request and deliver the files to her since I suspect that you probably didn't want the puppy squad taking over the courthouse."

"You do realize that we have 15 years of paperwork," she reminds the Judge.

"Yes, I know, Claire," he grins. "Lay it on me."

"O.K., then. I'll go get them. But, Judge Conner, you know it isn't going to make a difference. I think that Mr. Landis is just a lonely man who likes the attention. Why take that away from him? He wouldn't get to come in here and visit with everyone, get a hot meal and some company," Claire states.

"So that is what you think? He wants attention at Christmas time? A lonely guy?" the Judge raises his eyebrows.

"That's what most of us here in the courthouse believe. That and being a little bit 'off' in the head," Claire points to her head and winks. She walks to a wall of files and begins to rifle through huge drawers.

"There are a lot of files." Claire pulls numerous folders from drawers, placing them on her desk. "Yep, a lot of files," she repeats.

Claire walks to a closet where she pulls out an empty box and neatly stacks the files inside. "You know, each file, they pretty much say the same thing year after year, after year." She struggles to lift it and plops it on the counter.

"Yes, my dear Claire. I know." Judge Conner looks at the heavy box. "I doubt Sarah can carry this and walk three dogs. Claire, there is a luggage pulley in that closet. Can you please get it out?"

"Luggage pulley?" Claire stares at him.

"Just go in the closet, please. It's on the shelf in there," he points.

Claire walks back to the closet and looks up on the shelf where she spots the pulley and delivers it to him.

"Thank you," he extends the handle and places the heavy box on the pulley platform, securing it with cords.

"Claire, you can put my name on the sign out sheet for these. Give me two days. Sarah will return them," he orders.

"You've got it," Claire grabs a clip board and signs it for the Judge. "Have a good night, Judge Conner."

"Same to you, Claire," he waves and pulls the box out the door. "Here you go, Sarah." Sarah is sitting on the courtroom steps, petting the dogs. The portly man hands the luggage pulley to her. "Can you handle all of this?"

"Sure." She eagerly takes the handle and ties two of the leashes to it. "I appreciate this."

"So, what is so interesting about this case after all of these years?" he gives her a kind smile.

"I don't know. I guess he touches my heart. This very lonely man that reaches out for attention, but won't accept help during what should be the most joyous time of year intrigues me." Sarah pauses and looks off into the distance in deep thought. "You know he had a family once."

"Yes, I have heard that," Judge Conner nods his head.

"And now, there is no one. No family or friends. It makes me sad." She turns to look the Judge directly in the eyes. "It's just not right."

"No, Sarah, it's not right. I agree. I don't know what happened to Mr. Landis or why he does what he does. But, we need to respect his wishes and if he chooses not to accept help, then that is the way it shall be." He places his hand on her shoulder. "But, I know our girl Sarah, and if she wants to give this a try then, well, by all means I respect *your* wishes. If there is anything that I can do to help, you just let me know."

"Thank you." She turns and rallies the crew. With tails wagging and loud barks, the entourage heads down the street with the large box trailing behind them on wheels.

"You have two days with those, Sarah!" the Judge shouts. "Then you need to get them back to Claire!"

"I will! Thank you!" Sarah briskly makes her way back to her home just as dusk sets in. She enters her front door, juggling dogs and the files, as she manages to get all inside, unhooking the dogs from their leashes. She pulls off her tennis shoes, placing them next to the door and makes her way to the kitchen where she pours piles of dog food into three bowls, ready for her guests. They eagerly scarf down the generous portions while Sarah grabs a bottle of wine, wine glass, and makes her way back to the living room.

She crumples newspapers and pushes them under the new pile of logs waiting in the fireplace, lights kindling and ignites the logs and paper that quickly catch fire and blaze brightly. She pulls the large box of files next to the couch where she gets comfortable, snuggling with a thick, fuzzy throw. The tuckered pups make their way into the living room and gladly curl up in front of the crackling fire.

The mantle is strewn with garland weaved with tiny white lights and topped with mercury glass candle sticks. A dazzling nine foot tree stands in the corner, wrapped in glittery green ribbon, loaded with large pinecones and shiny silver ornaments. The room glows as shadows from the fire dance and the smell of burning logs lightly fill the air.

Sarah pours herself a glass of wine. "Let's see what we can find out about our Mr. Landis. OK, boys?" The pups stare at her, content to stay in their chosen spots.

Stacks of papers surround Sarah as she makes her way through the files. She sips her wine as she meticulously reads the details of each year's transcripts. Page after page, the scenario reads the same. A man places a lit Christmas tree on his roof and after numerous complaints is cited for violating building codes. After a court order to remove it, he ignores each request, ending up in jail at Christmas, fined or both. After Christmas, he then removes the tree which he carelessly stacks on the side of the house, only to repeat the act the next year. Sarah notices that through all of the information, there is something odd, something missing.

She pulls out all of the personal documents on Mr. Landis's house which she discovers is owned by an elderly Aunt who has allowed him to live there. The house is not in his name.

"No car or driver's license. That's right, he bikes everywhere." She continues to thumb through pages. "This is odd. There is no phone, email or contact person listed," she says out loud. "This is incredible. Outside of Christmas, this guy barely exists." The fire sparks and cracks. Doogie barks, as if confirming her statement.

"I agree, Doogie. What do you think Bo?" Bo walks to Sarah and puts his big head on her lap. His tail begins to wag. "Do you think we can help Mr. Landis?" The dog barks. "So do I," Sarah gives him a kiss on the face.

*Chapter Seven*

# Christmas Shopping Gets Interesting

It is dusk and the streets of Rosedale look like a picture perfect Christmas town decked out with sparkling lights and holiday music playing on outdoor speakers. Gas street lamps, wrapped in twinkling roping and red bows, flicker and glow. Sarah sprightly walks down the street, swinging numerous shopping bags and humming a holiday tune. Shoppers hustle past her, many tightly holding the hands of excited children who tug and try to escape to look at an interesting toy or item in a store window.

Sarah also occasionally stops to look into the decorated store windows when she comes upon the town's old Irish pub, beautifully decorated with old fashion trimmings on the door and windows. She peers in, her face pressed up against a large window when she spots John sitting at a table directly in front of her. He is with friends, laughing when he looks up, recognizes her and taps on the window, motioning for her to come in. She smiles, shakes her head, waves, and continues to walk. John darts out of the pub, slipping as he runs to catch up with her. He is carrying his coat, struggling to put it on as he runs.

"Sarah!" he yells. "It's treacherous out here! Don't make me slip and fall!"

"Very funny," Sarah half laughs and turns around to look at him. "That would be your ideal situation wouldn't it?"

"This is funny, isn't it? I mean running into each other like this? Sort of meant to be don't you think? Hey, why don't you come back inside and join me? You know, have a little Shepherd's pie, a nice Irish coffee or beer. It'd take the shivers off." He sees her hesitate. "Doing your Christmas shopping?" he looks at her arms clutching bags as they stand in the middle of the sidewalk. Shoppers dodge them, occasionally knocking into them.

"Yes. I don't have a lot of time left and I really need to get my shopping finished tonight. I have work to review and foster dogs waiting for me at home," she shares.

"No time for dinner? A big case coming up?" he cleverly smiles.

"I *am* working through the holiday. So, yes, I don't have much time to get everything done," she says slowly backing away when suddenly one of her bags tears and packages tumble to the ground. John grabs the boxes and gathers them in his arms.

"I hear you. I have to wrap up a case right up until Christmas, also," he says as he collects the items from the ground. "But, I thought it wouldn't hurt to take a small break. It's really nice being back here." He looks at her sweetly as he picks the ripped bag off of the pavement. "Come on. Let me help. I'll walk you to your next stop and we'll find you a bigger bag to put all of these in," he says, knowing that he won't be able to convince her to join him at the pub.

Sarah reluctantly agrees. "Sure, I guess that would be nice," she pauses when she realizes how ungrateful she sounds. "I'm sorry. I mean, that *would* be really nice. Thank you. I don't mean to pull you away from your friends, though."

John looks at the pavement and smiles to himself. "Believe me, they won't miss me. Besides, I would much rather spend a little time with you, even if it's just for a few minutes before you are off to finish your work." They turn and walk down the sidewalk, juggling the boxes and bags.

"Here," Sarah points. "This is my next stop. They should have big bags in here." They enter an elaborately decorated department store. A pianist in the entry area is beautifully playing holiday music. In front of them are displays of perfumes and cosmetics in glass cases. "I love this place." Sarah smiles then gazes around at the sparkling decorations like a child in wonderment. "My Mother used to bring me here when I was a kid and we'd enjoy the decorations and beautiful displays. We would sit and listen to the pianist, and she'd take me to lunch in the restaurant up on the second floor, then to see the store Santa," she smiles.

"Those must be wonderful memories," John says observing her now relaxed demeanor.

She looks into the glass case in front of them. A perfectly coiffed saleswoman walks up to assist them. Wafts of expensive perfumes fill the air. Sarah asks if she could have a large shopping bag for her packages and the woman happily pulls one out and helps to place the numerous packages in it. Sarah looks closer at the cosmetics and glittery compacts in the display case.

"Oh! My Mother would love this," she says pointing to a gold cosmetic bag with perfume and a jeweled compact. She looks at John, "She'd *never* buy anything like this for herself! I need to spoil her." She points to the item and asks the saleswoman to pull it out for her. "This is perfect." Sarah examines the bag and contents. "I'll take it! Can you wrap it for me, please? It's a gift."

The saleswoman nods and smiles, "You made a great choice," she takes the purchase to a counter where she begins to wrap it in holiday paper.

Sarah turns and looks at John. "So, do you have family here in Georgia?"

"No. My parents split up when I was very young. I was brought up by my Mother who never left New York. My family is scattered," he vaguely explains.

"Funny," Sarah cocks her head. "I never knew that about you. Are you joining any of them for Christmas?" Sarah asks.

"No, I plan on staying in town and visiting with friends," John says casually looking around the store.

"Oh," Sarah says suddenly feeling sorry for him, "Well I am sure you will have a wonderful time."

"Oh yeah, it's no big deal. I have a few holiday stops to make, maybe catch up on some work, and get some rest," he says, shrugging it off.

"You know, for some reason I thought that you were close to your family," Sarah says, regretting the bold comment, "I'm sorry, I didn't mean to be so nosey. We spent so many years together in school, and you were always flying back to New York. I just thought that you had a big family that you were close to."

"Well, that is partially true. I did fly back often, but not for the reasons you may think. I was actually taking care of family business. I needed to step in and handle some issues," he says looking uncomfortable.

"Oh, I'm sorry," Sarah realizes that she is making John nervous. She looks at him and smiles, "It's funny that for as much time we spent together through school, we never really talked about our families. In fact, we didn't really talk about our personal lives at all, did we?"

"I know. You are right. I guess we were kids just trying to get through school. Serious discussions never really seemed appropriate. Nor much fun," he smiles leaning on the counter looking directly into her eyes.

Sarah becomes noticeably uncomfortable at the attention and quickly hands the cashier her credit card. She leans over to pick up her bags at the same time that John leans over to grab them and they accidentally place their hands over one another's, their faces touching. They pause and begin to giggle like children.

"I can handle it, really," she says embarrassed.

"So are you sure you won't join me for a little bubble and squeak?" he beckons. "The food is really great. Perfect way to warm up on a cold night."

"I'm sure," Sarah responds, as she takes her credit card back along with the brightly wrapped gift from the cashier. She thanks the saleswoman and turns to John. "I'm sorry, John. I have a few more stops to make."

"Well, at least let me help you carry these back to your car," he offers.

"Sure," Sarah says, suddenly feeling compassion for him. "That would be nice."

They leave the store, bundling up as the chilly air hits them. John pulls her close to him and supports her as they walk down the busy street. They chat and laugh as they make their way to Sarah's car where they pile in the boxes and bags. She offers to drive him back to meet up with his friends and he gladly climbs into the passenger seat. As she pulls in front of the pub, John turns to her and stares.

"Your destination, Sir." She attempts to make light of his intense gaze. "Thanks again, John."

"It was my pleasure, Sarah. Thanks for the ride back. And if you get any down time over the holidays, it'd really be nice to see you," he leans over and kisses her cheek and lingers, catching her by surprise. "Think about it," he winks and opens the car door, pulling his coat close and flipping up his collar as he exits.

Sarah is taken aback and blushes as she watches him walk to the pub door. John turns to smile at her then disappears into the entrance. She laughs girlishly, shakes her head as she sits and stares at her steering wheel smiling to herself. She puts her car into gear and drives off with a big grin on her face, feeling happier than she had for a long time.

## Chapter Eight
# Wine and Old Wounds

Sarah makes her way up the porch steps of her home, fumbling to open the front door as she juggles her purchased treasures. She skids into the entry and drops everything on the floor as she pulls off her knit hat throwing it on an entryway chair, allowing her golden curls to escape. As she struggles to pull off her boots, she loses her balance and begins to fall over. She quickly steadies herself against a wall as the dogs greet her, barking and jumping.

"O.K., O.K., out in the yard, all of you," she orders. Without taking off her coat, she walks through the living room into the kitchen and opens the back door. The dogs gladly run into the backyard, playfully romping. Sarah heads to her couch where she plops down, sighing with relief. She begins to rub her sore feet, and laughs out loud, feeling unusually giddy and surprised at her own behavior.

The home is a classic bungalow with high ceilings, wood plank floors, and coved doorways. Large paned windows overlook the street and tall glass French doors divide the living and dining rooms. Sarah grabs several logs stacked in a basket, neatly piles them in the stone fireplace and stuffs newspaper underneath. She lights the pire and plops back on her couch when her cell phone rings. She digs to pull it out of her coat that is still tightly wrapped around her.

"Jessica! How are you my good friend? I just got back from doing my Christmas shopping and lit a crackling fire. What about you? What are you up to? Why don't you come on by," she offers. There is a knock on the door. "Just a moment, someone's here." Sarah walks to the door and opens it. There stands Jessica, leaning on the frame, cell phone in hand.

"That is a great idea, Sarah! I'll be right there," she teases. "What is this? You went shopping without me?" She places the back of her hand on her forehead and feigns acting shocked and insulted as she pushes her way past Sarah.

"Very clever. Yes, I did go shopping without you and I'll have you know that I did quite well," Sarah responds. "Please, come on in," she says sarcastically as Jessica walks past her and heads directly to the butler's pantry where she rifles through Sarah's wine cooler. "I have your favorite in there. You know where the glasses are," Sarah instructs her as she removes her coat. She picks up the shopping bags still strewn in the entry way, leaving Jessica in charge of uncorking a nice Burgundy and places her purchases in a heap in front of the couch.

"Make it two" Sarah orders, as she removes her coat.

"That was a given. You know I don't drink alone." Jessica returns to the living room with two full glasses and places them on the coffee table in front of them.

"And what inspired you to just pop in?" Sarah inquires.

"Oh, just missing my friend. Actually, I was in the neighborhood running errands and thought I'd check out your Christmas decorations and visit a bit." Jessica looks around the room. "It looks great, Sarah. I'm impressed. You actually got everything up and decorated. You just do it all, girl."

"Thank you, my friend," Sarah walks to the back door and lets the dogs in. They run, wildly into the living room and greet Jessica as Sarah laughs.

"Whoa, kids!" Jessica gives them all a pat and looks at Sarah who is beaming. "I am happy to see you in such good spirits."

"I'm in the holiday mood," Sarah responds, as she walks over to the Christmas tree and trips a switch launching a series of twinkling white lights. She quickly plops back on the couch and props her socked feet on the coffee table to warm them up from the heat of the fire. Sarah giggles and raises her glass of wine.

"To the best of friends and the happy holiday season," she laughs loudly. They raise their glasses.

Jessica stares at her suspiciously. "OK, what's up? Yes, this is a good wine, but it's not *that* special."

"What?" Sarah says, opening her eyes. "What do you mean?"

"What? You ask what? You are acting like a silly school girl. That's what. Did I miss something? Where were you earlier, really?" Jessica quizzes her with a serious look.

"I told you, last minute Christmas shopping. Seriously! Why?" Sarah asks.

"I don't know. You look. Well, you look weird or something." Jessica pauses and stares at Sarah, squinting at her. "You were just shopping? Really? What the heck did you buy that made you this giddy?" She begins to rifle through the shopping bags on the floor.

"Hey! Careful!" Sarah grabs a bag from her. "You may see something you aren't supposed to in there, like your gift!"

"Well, you should be stressed out like the rest of us. I happen to know that there is no sale that would have this kind of effect on you," Jessica states.

"Jessica, I *was* just shopping. I needed to get the rest of my Christmas gifts!" Sarah says not very convincing.

"Sarah, you don't get this happy over shopping. You don't even like to shop." Jessica stares at her. "Did you have a cocktail while you were out? Were they giving away margarita mix samples at that cookery store again? You remember the last time you sampled those!" Jessica says with her eyes wide and nodding her head as if she had hit on the answer.

"Can't someone simply be in the holiday spirit?" Sarah asks.

"Wait," Jessica says, sitting up straight. "Who were you with?"

"No one! I was shopping by myself," Sarah responds avoiding eye contact with Jessica.

Jessica leans over and gets close to her face, examining her. Sarah starts laughing as Jessica searches every inch for an answer.

"Oh my gosh! You were with a man! I have never seen you like this. Who in the heck did you run into? You may have been shopping alone, but you definitely ran into *someone* of the opposite sex! You are *way* too happy to have just been shopping or downing a margarita sample. Come on Sarah, confess! Was it a movie star? That hot trainer at the club?" Jessica talks excitedly as she continues to guess.

"No! Gosh, no! You are so wrong. No! Seriously," she says, emphatically.

Jessica looks at her without saying a word, takes a long sip of her wine and continues to stare with a big smirk on her face. She watches in silence as Sarah takes another sip of wine and squirms uncomfortably, pushing deeper into the couch cushions.

"OK, well I did run into someone. Just an old friend and I emphasize *just* a friend. Don't confuse my holiday spirit with anything else, Jessica," Sarah says defiantly.

"An old friend? What in the heck is that supposed to mean? Do tell!" Jessica presses her, leaning forward, dramatically batting her eye lashes.

"Gosh, I don't even want to tell you this," Sarah pauses and takes a deep sigh. "Don't make a big deal out of this, O.K? I ran into John. It was a total accident and he offered to help carry my packages to the car. That's it. No exciting story here, I'm afraid. Sorry to disappoint you."

"Really? John? *The* John? Hot, hot, John? Oh my gosh! My, my, my. For carrying packages to your car, you certainly seem to be in the happy zone. And, let's be honest. John has never been *just a friend*, my dear. I've known you way too long, don't forget. I know all of the dark secrets of your past, including study hall with John!" she says slyly.

"Jessica, don't go there again. We were study partners." Sarah throws her hands up in the air then grabs for her wine glass once again. "O.K., I'll put it out on the table for you. Here it is. John is a rich kid from New York, snobby law student, who studied corporate law no less, looking to make the big bucks regardless of whom he has to mow over to do it. He always dressed much better than any college student could afford, apart from the other rich kids. I have never had anything in common with him other than we did spend several years together studying. Yes, he is intriguing and entertaining," she says not very convincing as she picks up the wine bottle and pours herself another glass. Jessica pushes her own glass forward, demanding a pour. Sarah fills it then continues.

"And sure, John is cute," she continues to speak as if having a conversation with herself. "He's a bit charming in an arrogant sort of way. I am sure all of the women fall for that sort of thing, but I see right through it. John is out for John. I just don't see the attraction beyond the face and charm. He is just a friend and maybe at one point we were the best of friends, but that was a long time ago. Sure, he's brilliant at his career, but who wants to be with someone who directs his brilliance to negative means?" Sarah rambles. "Not to mention that he's been handed everything to him. He probably never had to work a day in his life, at least not that I know of. Sure he did do very well in school, and he worked hard on that, but I truly do not find him attractive in *that* sort of way."

Jessica puts her glass down on the cocktail table and looks intently at Sarah. "Girlfriend, for someone who claims he is just a friend, you are giving quite the commentary. Going by those glowing cheeks and run-on speech, I'd say there is some underlying attraction there that you aren't willing to either admit to, or you just aren't coming to terms with or both. Perhaps old feelings are resurfacing. Sounds like a love hate to me, or more love," Jessica says smiling like a Cheshire cat.

"And, Sarah darling, I'm sorry, but John is a nice guy. He defends companies and you defend petty criminals. It's really a matter of scale, isn't it? He just gets paid more. Somehow you think you are making a positive change, but I have to be honest, and you know this is true, not everyone agrees with that. You two are more alike than you'd like to admit. As for coming from a privileged family, watch who you say that around! It doesn't have to be a bad thing you know. There is nothing evil about money or that Trust fund that Granddaddy left me! There is a lot of good that you could do for your forlorn clients with money. So, what's wrong with liking him? What's the big deal?" Jessica asks.

"Oh, Jessica, I'm sorry. You know I didn't mean anything about the money comment. It's just that he has no conscience and puts money first. He is willing to do anything to make the big bucks. And, I didn't say I didn't *like* him. I just don't want to date him," Sarah blurts out.

"Oh," Jessica says surprised, "helping you with your packages and all, sounds like a marriage proposal for sure!"

"O.K., smart aleck. Point taken. But, he did want me to join him for a drink, and catch up," Sarah says trying to backtrack.

"OK, so he asked you to join him for a drink and a friendly visit between school friends? That's it? Wow, that is totally threatening. What a jerk!" Jessica says, pursing her lips, and rolling her eyes.

"OK, it wasn't a big deal. I was just trying to say," Sarah pauses, realizing that she had been rambling.

"I see where this is going," Jessica says, with a big smile, as she sits back into the couch with her wine glass cupped in both hands. "My, my, my, Miss Sarah," Jessica says putting on a heavy Southern accent.

"Jessica!" Sarah says, laughing and hiding her face in a pillow, "Stop it! You are making something out of nothing."

"Am I? You know you two were pretty inseparable," she reminds Sarah. "What happened?"

Sarah looks into the fireplace and becomes serious, pausing to think. "I don't know, really. He flew back to New York every chance he got. I didn't get to socialize all that much with him. John's always been very private about his family and personal life. For as much time as we spent together, I really can't tell you much about him. He seemed to always keep me from knowing too much. It was odd really.

We were so close but he never let me in, you know? So, when he got a job in New York, we lost touch. He just disappeared," she shares.

"Well it seems that he is willing to pick things up where he left off," Jessica declares. "You should go out with him!" Jessica leans forward. "Sarah, he is handsome, and successful, and he was always a lot of fun. You know, it might actually be good for you to spend time with a man instead of your girlfriends or the courtroom, or your furry friends," Jessica looks at the dogs. "Sorry guys. And who cares why he left. He's here. Go have fun."

"Alright, let's change the subject and look at the great gifts that I bought." Sarah puts her wine glass down and rifles through the piles of shopping bags. She pulls out boxes and gifts, stacking them on the couch and coffee table.

"OK, if you say so! Does this mean that I get to see my gift?!" Jessica asks.

"No you don't! You have to wait!" She slaps Jessica's hand. "Stay out of there you! I'll pull them out, thank you." They both laugh, as Sarah pulls the various purchases out.

"Hey, girlfriend," Jessica pauses and raises her glass. "I'm just glad to see you having fun and relaxing. Merry Christmas."

"Merry Christmas, my dear friend," Sarah responds. They continue to enjoy sorting through the gifts in the warm and glowing room.

*Chapter Nine*
# Look Who Santa Brought

The town is abuzz with excitement as the residents make their way to the center square where the official Christmas tree lighting ceremony is about to take place. Sarah, dressed in jeans and a ski jacket, makes her way to the festivities. She stops to purchase hot chocolate from a street vendor along the way when she spots her parents. Her Father is pushing Mrs. Costello who is in a wheel chair covered with a red blanket and wearing a Santa hat.

"Hello everyone! Hello, Mrs. Costello. I see that you are dressed for the occasion," Sarah tugs on her hat.

"Well, your parents kindly offered to take me to the lighting and I thought I'd be festive," she pulls her blanket tightly around her.

"Well, you look great. Mom? Dad? Shall we head down?" Sarah leads the way as the group heads to the end of the block where a huge tree stands. Food and hot beverage vendors surround the area, including carts of steaming chestnuts. The crowd thickens as the town comes out to celebrate. Carolers in red velvet period costumes carry candles, strolling and singing hymns. Families visit with one another while children noisily play and laugh with excitement. Sarah and her family walk to the front of the crowd and stop to speak to friends when Sarah spots Ellen, the Manager of the Animal Rescue.

"Ellen! Hello!" Sarah waves her over.

"Sarah, how are you? How are our pups? Enjoying their holiday stay with you?" she makes her way to Sarah.

"The crew is home resting right now. And, yes, they are having a great time romping in the yard, going on runs, and eventually collapsing in front of the fireplace."

"We are always so grateful for your help," she puts her hand on Sarah's shoulder.

"I really enjoy fostering them," Sarah pats Ellen's hand.

"Oh! Oh! Hello! Over here!" Ellen yells. "Oops, sorry," Ellen apologizes for yelling so abruptly. "There is that handsome man that helps out at the shelter."

Sarah turns around to see John walking toward them. Walking next to him, on a leash is a black Labrador retriever.

"Him?" Sarah gives a look of confusion. "I don't think . . . you must have the wrong," she mumbles.

"Ellen! Hey there!" John gives her a big smile and a wave.

"How is Baxter working out?" Ellen asks. John joins the women.

"You are fostering a dog?" Sarah asks.

"Well," Ellen interrupts, "John actually adopted Baxter."

"Adopted?" Sarah looks down at the sweet dog who calmly sits next to John.

"Yes. He has been helping us at the shelter and Baxter just took to him," Ellen laughs giddily and blushes, "like all of us have I'm afraid." She giggles.

"Well, all of you have made me feel so welcome, Ellen. And Baxter tugged at my heart. He is a great companion," he pats Baxter who licks his hand. "And the firm lets me bring him to the office!" John gives Sarah a smile.

"Oh . . . that is, uh, great," Sarah takes it all in.

"Yes, all of us at the shelter just *love* John," Ellen gushes. She leans over and gives John a hug, then hugs Baxter who licks her face.

"Shake, Baxter," John commands. Baxter offers Ellen his puppy paw.

"Oh, and he is already doing tricks! That is so sweet!" Ellen claps.

"Well, I need to go find my family," Ellen announces. "You have a wonderful night now, Sarah," she pats Sarah's shoulder again. "John, you have a Merry Christmas!" Ellen gives him another big hug and departs.

"Yes, Merry Christmas, Ellen," Sarah gives John a look. "I didn't know you were such a dog lover." She bends down and pets Baxter.

"Well, there is a lot you don't know about me," John gives her a big, Hollywood smile.

"I guess not," Sarah responds.

"Hello Mr. and Mrs. Wright," John waves to Sarah's parents who are nearby, speaking with another couple.

"Oh is that John? Hello there!" Mrs. Wright is delighted to see him.

"John! Come here young man," Mr. Wright waves John over and gives him a big handshake. "I hear that you've moved back to Rosedale! Welcome back. It's good to have you here."

"Yes, John, it is so good to see you," Mrs. Wright cheerfully greets him.

"Jessica!" Sarah shouts, waving to her friend that she spots making her way through the crowd. "Over here!"

"Ah, our friend Jessica," John waves at her.

"Hey there!" Jessica is out of breath as she runs to meet them. "I didn't want to miss the tree lighting. I was running late so I jogged here from my place."

"Thank goodness you are here," Sarah whispers in her ear.

Sarah pulls her close. "'You remember John."

"Yes, of course. Good to see you again," Jessica extends her hand and gives him a flirtatious smile. "Who is this guy?" Jessica leans down and pets the Labrador who is happy to receive so much attention.

"That would be Baxter," Sarah interjects.

"Well, hello Baxter," Jessica continues to fuss over the dog.

"Oh, there is Mayor Briggs," Sarah points. "We should be getting close to the big moment."

The Mayor looks around the crowd and spots Sarah, Jessica and John, and waves. Sarah waves back.

"John!" he shouts. John sees the Mayor who motions to him. "Come on. It's time! We're counting on you!"

"Oh, if you will excuse me," John says. "Baxter and I are on Santa duty."

"What?" Sarah asks.

"Oh, I am playing Santa after the tree lighting. I need to get suited up," he responds casually.

"And I suppose Baxter is your elf?" Sarah sarcastically responds.

"Well, yes, actually. He is. Aren't you Bax?" John pulls an elf hat out and puts it on Baxter's head. The dog appears to like it and barks.

"Come visit Santa, you two. You never know if he'll grant your wishes," John winks at Sarah.

"Thanks, but I think I have that under control," Sarah answers.

"O.K., if you say so! If you change your mind, you know where to find me! Come on Baxter," John turns to Mr. and Mrs. Wright. "Good bye Mr. and Mrs. Wright, and Mrs. Costello!" He gives a wave and leaves.

"Oh that John is just the sweetest man, isn't he Liz?" Mrs. Costello reaches out and holds Mrs. Wright's hand.

"Yes, he certainly is," Mrs. Wright agrees.

Jessica smacks Sarah in the arm. "Are you insane? The guy invites you to visit Santa and you 'have that under control'? Sarah, have you totally forgotten what it's like to flirt?"

"Oh, I know," Sarah shakes her head in regret. "He just gets to me, you know?"

"No, I don't know. What is your issue with him? Are you still harboring anger toward him?" Jessica prods.

Sarah takes a sip of hot chocolate. "No, it's not that. It's that he just pops back here and he's Mr. Popular all of a sudden."

"What? Mr. Popular? That's a bad thing? People obviously like him. You just don't like what he represents, but I am telling you again, Sarah, you are two peas in a pod. You really are," Jessica frowns.

"Whatever you say, Jessica," Sarah protests. "He is just so, so, so . . . snarky and all!"

"Snarky? Snarky? What does that even mean?" Jessica shakes her head in amusement.

Mayor Briggs steps up on a small platform in front of the large tree where he taps a microphone. "Testing, testing. I see some wonderful, familiar faces here tonight. I want to welcome all of you to the Rosedale Annual Tree Lighting! We have an especially beautiful tree this year, donated by the Parsons Family Farm," he points to a family standing nearby who look pleased to be stars at the ceremony. Everyone claps and cheers, patting Mr. Parsons on the back.

"As always, Santa will visit us immediately after the lighting, so kids, be sure to put in your Christmas wishes! And now, on to the purpose of this evening, the lighting of the tree. Will everyone count down with me?"

"10, 9, 8, 7, 6, 5, 4, 3, 2, 1 and . . ." the Mayor plugs a huge cord into a socket, illuminating the brilliant, graceful Christmas tree that lights up the entire square. The crowd cheers and screams, banging items, and whistling.

"I never get tired of this," Jessica smiles happily at the dazzling display.

Jessica pulls Sarah close and puts her arm around her. "Neither do I." They both stand in silence, staring at the tree.

"Now shall we go see Santa?" Jessica grabs Sarah's arm and leads her toward the base of the tree where John sits dressed as Santa with a padded out belly and thick beard. Baxter obediently sits next to him, dressed as an elf. He occasionally wags his tail and licks the face of a giggling child. A big "Ho! Ho! Ho!" belts out.

"No! No! No!" Sarah's voice pitch gets higher with every 'no.' "I am *not* going over there to talk to that man. The dog, maybe, but *not* Santa, 'er John."

"Bye Mr. and Mrs. Wright, Mrs. Costello!" Jessica continues to pull Sarah away. "Loosen up a bit and let's have some fun."

"Good bye dears!" Mrs. Costello waves along with Sarah's parents who are chatting with neighbors.

Jessica pulls on Sarah's arm and drags her through the crowd. "Here we come, Santa!" She laughs as they make their way to the long line of children anxiously waiting for their turn with Santa.

"Really, Jessica, this is ridiculous. And look at him. He's been here a month and already he is chummy with the Mayor, adopted a dog, and playing Santa? That is a very big role, as you know," Sarah continues to babble.

"Yes, I know," Jessica smiles. "Does all of this bother you?"

"All of what?" Sarah pauses to ask.

"This." Jessica points at John, the line of children, parents shaking his hand. "The fact that he is so popular. People like him. Is that so terrible?"

"Are you insinuating that I am jealous?" Sarah's mouth drops open.

"I don't know. Are you? I wasn't even thinking that. I was thinking that you want to hate him and you can't." Jessica stares at Sarah who avoids eye contact. "Hmmmm? Cat got your tongue?" Jessica teases.

"Let's change the subject. We are done here," Sarah grabs Jessica's arm and yanks her out of the line, dodging young children and parents.

"Oh come on!" Jessica protests.

"Yes, come on is right. We are going to get more hot chocolate," Sarah continues to pull Jessica to a vendor.

John looks up, as a child sits on his lap, and sees the women making their way out of the line. He beams a big smile through his thick, white beard. "Ho! Ho! Ho! Merry Christmas to all!"

*Chapter Ten*

# Fate and a Bad Battery

L ow, heavy clouds illuminated by a bright moon silently float by. On the lawn of the courthouse stands the elegant, brightly lit, 30 foot Christmas tree welcoming all who enter, oblivious to the dramas taking place inside. Dressed in a cherry red suit, Sarah stands at the head of the courtroom with her client, Mr. Hancock.

"Counselor Wright, you are looking quite festive this evening," Judge Conner compliments.

"Thank you, Judge," Sarah beams. "I am simply trying to bring a little cheer into the courtroom."

"Well, it is much appreciated," he clears his throat and speaks in a more serious tone. "As you know, Mr. Hancock, it is almost Christmas." He peers up from his paperwork at the weary, middle aged man dressed in jeans and a hooded, ratty, winter coat. "Mr. Hancock, do you have anywhere you can go tonight?"

"No your Honor," he sadly replies.

"Perhaps we can get you a hot meal, a warm bed, and friendly company. The Rescue Mission here in Rosedale always has nice meals and smiling faces. Counselor, if you will show Mr. Hancock to our front desk, we can make arrangements," the Judge says, giving Sarah a smile and a wink. She mouths "thank you" to him and walks the frail man into the hall and to the clerk counter where she gathers paperwork. She instructs her client to take a seat and wait.

"Thank you Miss Wright," the man says.

"Don't worry, Mr. Hancock. You will have a warm meal and a comfortable bed this holiday season, thanks to the kindness of Judge Conner," she responds, with a kind but professional tone.

"Still saving the world Miss Wright?" Sarah hears. She reels around to see John standing behind her.

"Still defending corporate villains?" Sarah retorts, and smiles.

"And exactly what goodness are you bringing into the world this evening? Putting criminals back on the street this holiday season?" he whispers once they get far enough away from her client.

"Everyone deserves a break, *especially* during the holiday season, don't you think? Even criminals," she answers quietly.

"Very good, Sarah! The woman has a sense of humor! And, I *totally* agree. It is always good to give someone a break. Therefore, I believe that in the spirit of giving you could find it in your heart to give an old friend a break this joyous holiday season. In fact, perhaps this very evening," he squints at her and cleverly smiles, "unless you have more Christmas shopping to do?"

"No, but I still have gifts to wrap and many other things I need to attend to," Sarah quickly excuses herself, trying to whisper so that her client doesn't hear. "I really need to get home."

"Right," John says, not surprised at her response.

"You don't have things you need to take care of?" Sarah asks.

"Finishing up here and nope, no plans, no obligations." As he is speaking, Sarah notices a man enter the courtroom whom she recognizes as her parents' troubled neighbor, Mr. Landis.

"Excuse me," she says distracted, "Give me a minute here. I need to check this out." John stands in the hallway, as he watches Sarah follow Mr. Landis into the courtroom. She takes a seat on a bench in the back. The thin, quiet man steps to the front of the room.

"Mr. Landis," the Judge says, as the man stares blankly at the floor, "How are you my friend?"

"The City of Rosedale vs. Mr. Landis," the bailiff announces.

Mr. Landis proceeds to the front of the courtroom, his head still hanging.

"It wouldn't be Christmas without my dear friend, Mr. Landis back here to visit us," Judge Conner examines Mr. Landis, waiting for a reaction.

"Merry Christmas, your Honor," Mr. Landis gives a shy smile, still looking at the floor.

"I see that we have yet again violated city building codes by placing a lit Christmas tree on your roof, and after an order to remove the tree you have chosen to keep it on your roof. Is this correct?" Judge Conner asks.

"Yes, your Honor," he responds.

"I suppose that you have no intention of stopping this ritual?"

"No, Sir. I won't be taking it down." Mr. Landis sheepishly replies.

"As you know, I must follow the law and fine you for this violation of building codes and set a court date for which time I will allow you to rectify this situation prior to your appearance. I won't incarcerate you this evening, but if you do not get that tree down, I can't promise that you won't spend Christmas Eve in our fine jailhouse. And, true to our yearly ritual, I will ask you if you care to share with me exactly why you feel it is necessary to place your Christmas tree on the top of your roof." The Judge looks intently at Mr. Landis and leans forward. "Mr. Landis, I really and truly would love to know why you continue to show up in my courtroom year after year. There are many other ways to display your Christmas enthusiasm, as you know. Perhaps you could place the tree on the front lawn, or porch, or inside your home where you can see it every night as I have suggested for many years."

"Your Honor, I don't mean disrespect. But, I like the tree on the roof, Sir," Mr. Landis calmly and slowly states.

"Well, Mr. Landis, in fifteen years, you haven't shared your reasons and I don't expect that you will tonight," he sighs. "Please go to the front desk where you will be given a court appearance date. You know that the tree must come down immediately or it will be taken down for you," Judge Conner says. "And, Mr. Landis," he pauses and smiles, "have a very Merry Christmas," he leans forward and looks the man in the eyes. "I hope that I won't see you next Christmas, at least not in this courtroom."

"Merry Christmas, your Honor," Mr. Landis quietly replies.

By this time, Sarah has made her way to the front of the courtroom. "Your Honor," Sarah disrupts the proceedings. "May I approach the bench?" Judge Conner raises his eyebrows and waves for her to step forward. "Your Honor," Sarah keeps her voice low. "As you know, I am familiar with Mr. Landis's case and although I know you may not agree, I would like to offer my services, pro bono." She pauses. "Sorry, but I just have to give it a try."

"Ms. Wright. . . .Sarah," Judge Conner begins, speaking softly so that the courtroom attendees cannot hear him, "if Mr. Landis wants your assistance, then I will not stand in the way. However, I must remind you that he has made an appearance in this courtroom every Christmas for many years. This is not a criminal case. Are you sure this is something that you want to put your efforts into?"

"Your Honor, I have witnessed Mr. Landis's holiday display for years and am aware of the serious safety and building code violations, not to mention the dissatisfaction of the neighbors and the town. I would be happy to offer my services to help him in this matter," she compassionately states.

"Mr. Landis, please approach the bench once again," Judge Conner orders the man who is still standing at the front of the courtroom. "Attorney Wright would like to offer her services pro bono on this case . . . in other words, free of charge. Would you like to accept this gracious offer?" he asks.

Mr. Landis carefully thinks and then answers. "Your Honor, and Miss, I appreciate the offer, but I don't need the help," he states in a kind, but firm manner.

"Are you sure that you fully understand what Ms. Wright is offering?" Judge Conner asks.

"Yes Sir," he responds, "I do understand that services would be for free and I appreciate it. But, I'll be keeping the tree on the roof for now."

"We will respect your wishes. I know that you are well aware of the consequences by not abiding by the rules. You may go now," Judge Conner states.

Sarah looks at Judge Conner with great disappointment. The Judge nods his head and motions her with his hand to leave the court-room. John, who had been watching from the back of the room, slips into the hallway.

Judge Conner stands. "Attention, everyone! I invite all employ-ees and visitors to congregate in the hallway for holiday food and drinks." The bailiff declares the court proceedings adjourned. "We may even have a special appearance by a certain jolly man," the Judge hints.

Sarah packs up her briefcase and exits into the hallway where she finds John sipping punch. A portable table covered with a paper table cloth decorated with pictures of bells and ornaments is stacked with food and drinks where the court employees are gathered. Next to it stands a brightly decorated fake Christmas tree with multi-colored, blinking lights. Courtroom employees, attorneys, defendants, and plaintiffs are laughing and speaking loudly as Christmas music plays from a portable stereo.

"Did you figure out how to rescue the evil Christmas tree of-fender?" John teases, taking a bite from a Christmas cookie.

"Very funny, John. That sweet man places a lit Christmas tree on the roof of his home every Christmas and every Christmas the neigh-bors complain and every Christmas he ends up here. He is harmless and all alone."

"This makes him an ideal case for you, Sarah. A perfect 'fix it' kind of 'save the world' client!" John states.

"Except he won't let me," Sarah declares.

"Really?" John is surprised.

"Yes. I offered. But, he wouldn't accept it."

"I am sure he has his reasons." He sees that she is deep in thought and takes a more serious tone. "Well, he is missing out on the Clarence Darrow of 'do gooders.' I am sure if he gave you a chance, you would do incredible things for him, Sarah." She smiles. "Sarah Wright, you're a good person and a good attorney," John says, placing his punch glass down. "You certainly stick with your beliefs," he pauses, "and I have to admit that I like that," he smiles in a flirting manner staring at her intensely. Sarah becomes uncomfortable.

"Ho! Ho! Ho!" loudly bellows from a jolly Santa who enters the hall, handing out gifts. The portly man walks up to them. "I see you two have met," he teases.

"A fine job you've done with Ms. Wright, Judge Conner. She is an excellent attorney," John comments.

"Santa, young man, Santa is the name!"

"Oh, right. Santa," John laughs.

"Well, I can't take credit for that, John. She certainly has earned it. It was I who was privileged to have such an ambitious, bright intern. And, I have heard that you have accomplished much yourself since you left our fine little town. Your work is impressive. I hear that you are heading up the corporate law division down the street and came on as a full partner," the Judge compliments. "With an opportunity like that, I can understand why you gave up the bright lights of New York." Sarah looks at John with surprise. "Oh, John didn't tell you Sarah? He is quite the force in his firm. Quite an accomplishment, especially for someone of his age, don't you think?" he adds.

"No, he didn't mention it," she says still showing her surprise. Sarah gives John a look. "Congratulations, John. That is wonderful," she says sincerely and continues to stare.

"I guess," he smiles shyly and shrugs his shoulders.

"You guess? That is very impressive," Sarah shakes her head.

"It is indeed," Judge Conner says. "John, it is good to have you here. I look forward to hearing more of your cases. Oh and Sarah, he's not such a bad guy outside of the courtroom you know." The Judge turns and whispers in John's ear, "I think that persistence will be required. She loves a charity case you know."

"I am up for the challenge," John whispers back.

"I thought that you might be." The Judge grabs John's arm and grasps his hand, giving him a strong hand shake then loudly says, "Now I must scoot. The reindeer are waiting! Merry Christmas to you and yours. I look forward to seeing you both perform miracles!" He smiles as he turns and speaks with people in the hallway, shaking hands, and laughing with a big booming voice.

Sarah looks at the big clock on the wall, "I really should be going."

"Please, let me walk you to your car," John quickly sees his opportunity. "It's getting slick out there. I'll just grab my coat and say 'good bye' to a few folks."

"Yeah, that would be great. Thanks," Sarah agrees.

John quickly walks over to a chair where his coat lies. He puts it on and grabs his briefcase before Sarah can change her mind. He chats with court staff as he heads toward the door, wishing them a Merry Christmas.

Sarah sees the women fawning over John and shakes her head, chuckling to herself, as she walks back into the now dark court room to retrieve her own coat and briefcase. As she walks to the front of the room, she sees a bright light glowing from Judge Conner's chambers. The door cracks open slightly and there is a blinding sparkling light emanating from the room. Sarah walks to the door and peeks in.

"Judge Conner?" She looks around the room that is glowing from an unknown source. It is much brighter than the light that emanates from the small Christmas tree in the corner, and illuminates the space like a blazing fire. "Are you in here?" Sarah sees a large figure in the room, but the light behind it is so bright that she can not see the figure's face. It appears to be the Judge in his Santa suit.

"Judge? Is that you? I thought you were in the hallway," she states, squinting to see the figure before her.

"Sarah, I forgot to give you your Christmas gift," the man says.

"Oh gosh, Judge Conner, you didn't have to do that!" Sarah says still sheltering her eyes from the blinding glow. He walks to the Christmas tree, pulls something brilliant off of it and hands it to Sarah. It is a beautiful, sparkling star. It has an energy and light that causes her to react in amazement. "This is beautiful!" she exclaims, "Thank you so much," she looks at him with some confusion.

"It's a special gift Sarah. You'll know what to do with it," he pauses. "I hope that you will keep your faith in miracles. But, Sarah, make sure that you keep your heart open not only to others, but to yourself," he adds with a kind voice.

"I'll try, Judge Conner, although I am not really sure what you mean," she replies.

"You will one day. I don't want you to miss out on the best miracle of all. To love others, you must open your heart and allow yourself to be loved."

"OK, Judge Conner. I'll do my best," she begins to feel uncomfortable with his comments. "Thank you for the beautiful Christmas gift." Sarah is amazed at the beauty of the star with a magnificent glow that appears to be self-generated.

"You are welcome, Sarah. Merry Christmas," he replies.

Sarah is mesmerized with the star and when she looks up, she can no longer see the Judge. She looks around the room unable to find him anywhere. "Merry Christmas," she says, her voice trailing off as she continues to look around for the Judge. When she walks back into the dark courtroom, Judge Conner's chambers dim. She shakes her head in confusion, grabs her coat and briefcase, and exits the room, still hypnotized by the beauty of the star she holds in her hand.

"You took quite a long time in there. Are you O.K.?" John asks as Sarah approaches. She looks around and sees that Judge Conner is no longer in the hallway.

"It must have been him. That was strange," she whispers to herself.

"What's that?" John asks.

"Judge Conner. Did you see him?" Sarah asks.

"Yes. He left right after he spoke to us. I saw him walk out to the parking lot in his Santa suit," John points to the door.

She looks down again at the star in her hand.

"Nice star," John comments. "Let's get going. Everyone is clearing out."

"O.K., sure," she shakes her head, and stares at the courtroom door. "Yeah, let's get going." Sarah puts her boots on and places her high heels in a large bag she carries, carefully storing the beautiful star inside it. "Ready," she tells John. John puts his arm out for Sarah to take as they begin to descend the slippery stairs, but she does not take it. As soon as she takes her first step, she begins to slip and yelps. "Oh!" She grabs John, who gladly catches her and slowly guides her down. "I didn't realize it would be that slick," she says surprised. "Thanks for saving me from cracking my tailbone!" she laughs.

"It's my pleasure," John laughs. "It's a tailbone worth saving!" He places his arm around her, making sure that she is stable. Sarah does not resist. They safely reach her car which she unlocks, placing her briefcase and purse in the passenger seat. Everyone in the courthouse is quickly making an exit. The bailiff and security guard are the last to leave, locking the court building doors.

"Thanks, John," Sarah says as she situates herself in the drivers seat and buckles up.

"Sarah, I know that it's a couple of days away, but if I don't see you beforehand, Merry Christmas," John says as he leans down and kisses her forehead. "Be careful now, and drive slowly. I mean it." He gives her a long, caring look before he walks to his car nearby. He looks back and smiles. Sarah watches him wanting to respond, but finds herself frozen.

She stares at her steering wheel, and bangs her head lightly on it several times. "Stupid! Stupid! Stupid!" She looks back over at John who hops into his car and quickly starts it, waiting for his blowers to clear the fog off of his windshield. Sarah sits in her car with the keys in the ignition, turning it several times only to hear clicking. Seeing the problem, John walks to her car and knocks on her window as she continues to turn the key and pump the gas pedal.

"You know you can't do that with these cars. You'll just flood it. Sarah, your battery is dead," John yells, knocking on the driver side window. Sarah opens the car door when she realizes that her window won't open.

"What?" she says, looking flustered.

"May I assist?" John leans in the car. "I don't have jumper cables, but I'm great at phoning AAA." He looks around the parking lot that is now completely empty as the last car pulls away. "No one else is going to be around tonight. I can stay here until they arrive. The courthouse is locked up now."

Sarah continues to turn the key with no response. She takes a big breath and looks at him. "Sure. Thank you. I'd appreciate that. It's so darned cold out here."

"Since it's a bit chilly out, well since it's *very* chilly out, may I suggest that perhaps it would make sense to camp out in a warmer environment while we wait for assistance?" He gestures to the rustic bar across the street from the parking lot. Sarah looks over at a tiny, wooden building with bright Christmas lights twinkling in the windows. She hesitates. "Come on, Sarah. Let's stay warm while I call for assistance. You can have that cocktail that you promised to have with me. Look," he points at the windows on the restaurant that have a direct view of the parking lot. "We can see the car from there." He looks at her with a puppy dog face. "Now don't be afraid."

"I'm not afraid!" she insists.

"Really?" He leans closer to her. "For a hot shot, fierce attorney, you are acting pretty timid."

Sarah looks at the keys in the ignition, the dark courthouse, and the glowing, friendly restaurant. "I never really noticed that place," she says with a sigh and begins to relax. "John, I appreciate you staying with me," she turns and looks deep into his eyes. "Really, thank you."

"Well, take my arm, little lady and I will guide you to warmth, food, and shelter," he teases. Sarah giggles. He helps her gather her items and secures the car. They walk out of the parking lot and across a side street, arm in arm, laughing and discussing the day as they make their way to the cabin-like building.

They enter a warm room that glows with twinkling, colored Christmas lights strewn around windows, on a small tree, and over the bar. Each table has a candle on it. Holiday music is playing and customers are laughing and happily carrying on conversations. A small, stone fireplace crackles and blazes. Next to a window near the fireplace is an empty, cozy booth.

"Let's sit there," Sarah points. "We can see the car from that window." They slide into the booth. Sarah is shivering and pulls her coat close around her. John makes a call on his cell phone, requesting service for Sarah's car.

"It may be a while," he announces. "Due to the colder weather and holiday activities, there seems to be somewhat of a backup."

"Of all times for my car to die." She shakes her head. "So much to get done. Just my luck."

"No, my luck," John laughs.

An older waitress with a kind face greets them. "Happy Holidays folks. What can I get you two on this chilly evening? Two Irish coffees perhaps?"

Sarah removes her gloves, rubs her hands together and blows on them to warm up.

"How did you know?" John smiles.

"That sounds perfect," Sarah says happily.

"Make it two," John announces.

"Two piping hot Irish coffees coming up," the server responds and heads to the bar to place their order.

Sarah's cheeks become flushed as she begins to warm up. She looks around the restaurant with its beautiful, log walls, heavy ceiling beams, and rustic décor. Tiny lamps are lit on small tables that sit next to two club chairs parked in front of the fireplace. A young couple sits in them, sipping red wine and having a conversation. An elderly couple is eating their dinner at a small table, saying nothing. The older gentleman takes his wife's hand across the table and they smile affectionately at one another.

John laughs and shakes his head.

"What?" Sarah looks at him. "What is so funny?" she smiles.

"Oh, I just enjoy seeing you relaxed and happy, like when we used to hang out together. You were a lot of fun," he smiles.

"Ah, a hint of vulnerability! You like that!" Sarah is amused.

"Yeah, I have to admit that I do. You are such an independent and guarded person. I forgot how carefree and happy you were once. I see a hint of that. It's nice," he says.

"Wow, is it that bad? I '*was*' a lot of fun?" She pulls off her white, knit cap, leans back and throws her mane of hair off of her face. "Have I become that serious? And guarded? I don't like that description at all."

"Well, it's been a while since we spent time together. You were a silly, fun girl then," he replies.

"Ouch. And now?" she looks at him sadly.

"Now, you are so focused on everything and everyone else, that I don't see the Sarah that took the time to laugh once in a while," he takes her hand.

"There isn't much time it seems," she looks down at their hands, and slowly pulls hers away, pretending to need it to push her hair back. "I suppose there is some truth to that. I'd hate to think that I am no longer fun. In all honesty, outside of anyone connected to my work and charity activities, Jessica is the only person I really spend much time with, I'm afraid."

"Well that makes it easy," John comments as the waitress returns with two mugs of Irish coffee topped with overflowing cream.

"Easy?" Sarah cocks her head and looks at him with a questioning face.

"Yeah. You can tell Jessica and your dogs anything. No challenges, right?" he blows on the steaming cup.

"And what challenges would those be?" Sarah takes a spoon and eats a big scoop of cream.

"You know. Dating, emotions, attachment, or anything that may interfere with your program?"

Sarah smiles slyly and nods her head. "I see. My program." She pauses and eats another spoonful of cream. "You know, there is so much that I don't know about you, John. Like you said, we spent so many years together, studying, and helping each other get through school, yet, I don't know some of the simplest things about who you are outside of that."

"What is it that you don't know?" John asks.

"Well, like anything about your childhood, your family. You told me you were flying back to New York to help your Mom. I was never aware that your family was going through difficult times. I never even knew that your parents had split when you were young," she adds.

"What, exactly, would you *like* to know?" he asks.

"I don't know. I don't mean to pry. I guess I don't really need to particularly know any details so much as I am just wondering *why* we don't know about each other. You know, like real friends do," she says. "Like why you left town and why you suddenly appeared without so much as a phone call."

"I suppose we were both so driven. Always studying, trying to be our best, internships, working, *always* working," he says taking a big sip from his steaming mug.

"I think you are right. We are alike that way. Not making time for much else. We never took the time to have fun outside of the library or classrooms. It's like I never looked around at even simple things. Like all of the time that I have spent in the courthouse across the street, and I've never even noticed this place," Sarah shares.

"Well," John says, "perhaps you *should* take a little more time off to look around and enjoy yourself. That's Margaret in the kitchen cooking, her husband Gus at the cash register who also cooks and makes a mean burger I might add, and their daughters Barbara and Leslie, and cousin Jennifer are serving the tables and bar customers," he lifts his mug to one of the gals behind the counter and she waves back at John.

"Now how would you know that?" Sarah questions.

"Well, let's just say that I have spent more than a couple of evenings and a few holidays at the Horse Shoe Grill," John shares.

"Really?" Sarah inquires.

"Yeah. Before I moved back to New York, I spent a lot of time in the courthouse, just like you. There are many nights that I found the comfort of this place. I didn't have my family here like you," John shares.

Sarah blows on her mug and sips through the white foam on the top, unknowingly collecting a white mustache on her upper lip. John leans forward to wipe it off, startling her.

"I don't bite, Sarah." John leans back and frowns.

"I'm sorry, John. It just took me by surprise. It's just that I . . . I, well," she stutters.

"You haven't been out with a man in a while?" he smiles.

"Yeah, I have to admit that would be the case. I guess I am just a bit jumpy," she responds.

"Don't feel bad. I have been a bit gun shy myself in that department," he shares without elaborating. "So, why is it that such a beautiful woman doesn't make time for dating?" He looks at her and then rethinks the statement. "I'm sorry, Sarah. I don't mean to pry."

Sarah gives him a sheepish look. "No, no. It's fine. Actually, there is no one. It's been my choice. I prefer not to complicate my already hectic life. That may sound a bit stupid and perhaps shallow, but it's just what I prefer, at least at this point in my life. And you? Might I assume the same applies to you? I mean, that there is no one special in your life?"

"You would be right on both counts. No one special and nothing complicating my already complicated life, as you put it," John says, holding up his mug.

"Well, I guess I am not so nutty. There are others like me. My friends and family, of course, give me a hard time. But, I am happy," she explains.

They clink mugs. "Here's to not complicating our lives any more than they already are," John toasts.

"Yes, here's to not complicating our lives," Sarah enthusiastically agrees. They both take a long drink and then find themselves in a lingering stare. "So, I have a personal question," she says in an effort to break the awkward silence.

John squints his eyes in a playful way, "Is this going to be painful?" he laughs. "OK, I'm ready . . . go ahead." He grabs the table as if to brace himself.

"Well, I remember when we were in law school and you seemed so . . . well, hopeful and positive. I never imagined that you would be representing the . . . you know, the 'not so good guys,'" she says in a very sweet voice.

"Ah, go ahead and just say it. The bad guys! Evil corporations. Worse! Pharmaceutical corporations! Knowing your view on the world and being such an *incredibly* positive person, I am sure you must think the worst of me," he says in a light manner.

He looks off in the distance and thinks for a moment. "Don't think there wasn't a lot of thought put into choosing what path I was going to take." He leans over the table closer to her. "I didn't want to be a prosecuting attorney for sure. I enjoy the research and the debate, so defense was definitely of interest." He pauses again.

"Sarah, our job is to win for our clients whether they have big bank accounts or small. We both manipulate and distort the truth to accomplish that. I just get paid more. Is that so wrong?"

"Well . . ." Sarah looks out the window at the empty parking lot where her car sits. "I think that everyone is entitled to pursue their own passion. It's a personal decision, so I don't want you to think that I am judging you."

"Ah, but I sense somehow that is exactly what is going on here. And you?" John asks.

"Me?" she is jolted from deep thought.

"Yes, you. What was your motivation? Why did you pursue this career path?" he quizzes.

"This may sound silly to you, but I'd like to think that I can make a difference. Maybe get them to a place where we'll never have to see them in a courtroom again. Give them back hope. You know, I think it's possible. I know that may sound corny, but it's what motivates me. Does that make any sense?"

John looks at her with a big, warm smile. "Sarah, there are no miracles. I think it is a very nice gesture on your part, but I don't have a whole lot of faith in . . . well, very much," John states very matter-of-fact.

"Really? That saddens me, John. Everyone should believe in miracles." Sarah shakes her head then smiles. "So I guess a Christmas Miracle is out of the question, huh?" She laughs.

"Yep, pretty much. Even at Christmas," John smiles. "Don't get me wrong. I envy your faith in humanity and all. But, I don't hold out much hope for it, personally. I think that what you do is a lot of work for limited results, if any. Like your Mr. Landis? There is a guy who needs a miracle. Getting arrested year after year for putting a tree on the roof? That's a new one and pretty crazy! Someone needs to show him that life can be a lot less complicated simply by keeping his Christmas enthusiasm under control. There are a lot more important things for us to be doing every day in the courtroom than getting some guy to stop pounding a Christmas tree onto his roof, don't you think?" he asks.

"I don't know. He lives across the street from my parents and when I was a teenager, he started putting a Christmas tree on the top of his roof, all decked out. He is a real recluse. I think that somehow celebrating Christmas with his big, sparkly tree brings some joy to him, or maybe just a lot of attention during what might be a lonely time of year. I don't know why he does it. Maybe he's lost his mind, but I don't find anything wrong with it. I think it's pretty harmless, don't you? I was hoping he'd allow me to help him."

"Well, he comes back every year Sarah. It seems like a lot of effort for a situation that doesn't make sense in the first place, but perhaps next year you can help the poor guy and put his neighbors out of their misery," John says sarcastically.

"Yeah, maybe," she says with a soft smile on her face.

"Well, here's to Christmas 'outside' of the courtroom," John cheerfully toasts. "Hey, look!" John shouts, looking out the window to the parking lot where Sarah's car sits. John points as the AAA truck pulls into the courthouse parking lot, lights flashing, and backs up to her car. He throws money on the table, and shouts 'Merry Christmas' to the wait staff who all wave and shout a "Merry Christmas." The two grab their coats and pull them on, wrapping them close to their bodies. John puts his hand out and Sarah grabs it as they exit the door. They slip and slide across the street, approaching the car where the AAA driver has the hood up.

"We'll just let that charge up for a few minutes," the driver says. "But, I think that it is really dead, Miss. I think that you may need a new battery. It may not start again tomorrow," he explains. "I have a new one if you want to go ahead and replace it now."

"Thank you, yes, let's do that," she says as she opens the car and tries to start it again. There is no response.

"Not a problem at all," he kindly responds. "I am happy to help. Care for a cup of coffee?" he asks, pointing to a flask he has sitting on the front seat of his truck.

"Thank you," Sarah says, surprised. "That is really nice. I'm all set, thanks."

"I'll just get to putting the new battery in then," he unhooks the cables.

Sarah turns to John who motions her to his car. "Hop on in for a few." He starts his car and opens the passenger door for Sarah. She climbs in.

"Well, this certainly has been an unexpected start to the holiday season," he laughs.

"Yes, it has," Sarah responds. "I can't thank you enough for taking care of me. It was really nice spending time with you, John. It really was."

John looks down and pauses as the heating vents blow and the windows begin to clear. "Sarah, I hope you know that I never meant to be so distant with you in school. I mean, I didn't mean to be so mysterious." He looks at her and smiles. "I really like you. Now that I am back here, in Georgia, I hope that I can get to know you better, beyond the books, our careers and the serious stuff. I'd like to get to know Sarah Wright, the person."

"Really? " Sarah says looking a bit surprised, but pleased. "Well, I guess I could live with that," she smiles sweetly. "That would be nice."

They both are silent. John looks at her, touches her face and smiles. There is a knock on John's window, interrupting the moment.

"You're all set!" the AAA driver yells. "I have her running."

Sarah gets out of the car and hands him her AAA card. "This is much appreciated and I hope you have a wonderful Christmas," she responds.

"If you have any more problems, you just give us a call." He takes the card, writes down the numbers, and hands it back. "Have a Merry Christmas now!"

"Thank you. Same to you," Sarah says as she walks back to her car, and places her purse and briefcase back in the passenger seat. She turns around and looks at John who has gotten out of the car and stands beside her.

"Hey," she smiles. "Thanks so much for making sure I got out of here safely."

"Not a problem. I enjoyed it," he answers.

"Yeah," she smiles, "I did too. I'm sort of glad that the car didn't start," she says.

"So there is hope for the evil corporate attorney?" He teases.

"Hope?" Sarah gives him a slight smile. "Yeah, there is always hope, John. That is assured."

She gets in her car, pulls on her seat belt and waits as the engine warms up. John walks past his car, across the street and back into The Horseshoe Grill. She stares curiously, then puts the car in gear and makes her way out of the parking lot.

## Chapter Eleven

# An Impossible Assignment

S arah is dressed in a black suit and heels, filing through papers as she sits in her office at the law firm. She clicks away on her computer keyboard, pauses, and sighs, staring out the window. After a few moments, she stands, hands on her hips and looks around the office at the stacks of books and papers. She grabs a file, and stuffs it in her large purse before walking into the hallway and the office next door. She pokes her head in the door of her colleague's office. "Jim, I'm going to take a breather. I'll be down the street at The Pot Hole."

"You'll love today's special. Mushroom and meatballs pot pie," he announces, not looking up from his computer screen.

"Great. Thanks, Jim. That's good to know," Sarah shakes her head, smiling, and walks out of the office, down the elevator, and exits on the street level. She makes her way past storefronts until she reaches an old, brick building with a wooden sign swinging over the door, "The Pot Hole." On the window is a stencil of a large, steaming pot pie.

Sarah enters and makes her way to the back of the café to the 'take out' counter. As she examines the menu, she looks to the wall beside her where a large chalk board lists various specials and favorites. Sarah notices that in a far corner of the room sits old lady Bell at a table, eating. With her sits John, with Bell's fat terrier, Emma on his lap. He is feeding Emma part of his pot pie, while Bell stuffs herself with her own pie.

"Well, I'll be," Sarah is taken aback.

"Sarah? Did you say something?" A man from behind the 'take out' counter asks. "Can I get you something?"

"Yeah. Hey, Charlie, what is Bell doing here?" she asks.

"Oh, having lunch with Mr. Rivera. She and Emma love having their pot pie lunch with him," he shakes his head happily.

"Having 'their' lunch with him? I don't think I've ever seen Bell eat much less heard her speak! Is this some kind of ritual?" Sarah continues to stare at Bell and Emma in amazement as they happily scarf their meals.

"Well, it's a fairly regular thing now that Mr. John is in town. He meets her here a couple of times a week and buys them lunch. I'm not sure what they talk about, but I hear a lot of laughter, and a few barks, too." Charlie laughs. "It's amazing, isn't it? She sure seems to like that young Mr. Rivera."

Sarah's mouth is slightly open as she stares, careful not to let John see her. She moves back around the corner to conceal her presence and watches the endearing scene.

"Can I get you anything, Sarah?" Charlie asks.

"No, Charlie. I think I'm good. Thanks. I think I'll just have lunch at the courthouse." Sarah watches a bit longer and quietly leaves through the kitchen and out the back door. She shakes her head in amazement as she returns to her office where she packs up her briefcase and makes her way to the courthouse.

Sarah sits in the courthouse cafeteria with a cup of coffee and a Panini along with legal documents she is reviewing in preparation of her case when she looks up to see John in the hallway, getting on an elevator. She quickly collects her documents and stuffs them into her satchel, tossing the half eaten Panini in the garbage and runs to catch the elevator just as the doors begin to close.

"Well hello stranger," John says noticeably happy to see her. Sarah acts as if she didn't know that he had gotten on and responds in a surprised manner.

"Oh, hello! This is a surprise!" she says.

"Yes, a real surprise to see another attorney in a courthouse isn't it?" he says sarcastically.

"Yes, a real shocker," Sarah responds, feeling a little silly and nervously adjusts her suit jacket. "Litigating an important case?" she asks.

"I'm supposed to be in there right now, in fact, but I am running late," he says looking at his watch as he loosens his tie and blots perspiration from his forehead.

"You must be the 'Golden Boy,' John," she comments.

"Golden Boy? Why is that?" he responds.

"Well, if I was late as often as you, I would be washing Judge Conner's dishes for a year, mowing his lawn, grounded for life," she smiles sheepishly at him, "or at least have some serious repercussions. He doesn't tolerate tardiness," Sarah boldly states.

John gives Sarah a serious look. His dimples appear, making him adorably attractive. "I know, I know. Believe me, I am well aware that I'm pushing my luck." The elevator doors open and John immediately bolts. He begins to run down the hall toward the courtroom, stops abruptly and turns around. "Talk to you after court?" he yells back to Sarah as she steps out of the elevator. She nods her head with a smile, entertained at the thought that John may be in deep waters with Judge Conner. John sprints to the courtroom door, slowly opens it and slides in. Judge Conner looks up and sees him sneak in, as he is speaking to another attorney. As he finishes, he looks up at John.

"Counselor Rivera, would you please approach the bench?" he commands sternly.

John cautiously walks to the front of the room and stands before the Judge, looking at the floor.

"Counselor, I don't need to tell you that you are late once again," he says.

"Yes, your Honor, I apologize. I ran into unavoidable traffic. I truly am sorry," John says.

"It appears that there are more traffic issues for you than everyone else, Mr. Rivera. I am sure that you are well aware that you disrupt

THE ROOFTOP CHRISTMAS TREE

my court proceedings, inconvenience a lot of people starting with those connected to your own case, and every other case that we see on those special days because you disrupt the fluidity of the schedule, creating a backlog and extra work for our clerks who must juggle the time slots to accommodate your poor planning," he says without taking a breath.

John's eyes are big as he stares at the Judge in surprise, "Uh, yes, your Honor, I suppose that is true. That is not my intention, your Honor. It truly isn't," he responds.

"Mr. Rivera, I need to put some thought into this. Please check with the clerk to find a time when I can speak with you today. I feel that I must administer a reprimand that may help you to better prioritize your schedule young man," he announces.

"Excuse me your Honor. I'm sorry. Did you say *reprimand?*" John stutters.

"Yes, John, I did. It is time to implement consequences for your actions that may aid you in your time management. This is a habit that is not welcome in this courtroom. Perhaps I can *encourage* you to get an earlier start from now on," the Judge smiles.

"Oh," John says slowly, pausing, and looking nervous, "Of course your Honor." He looks at the Judge still concerned about the potential 'reprimand.'

"Mr. Rivera" the Judge smiles with satisfaction, "I shall see you shortly."

"Yes Sir," John responds. "I mean yes, your Honor."

The Judge smiles, pleased at John's concerned reaction. "You may go now."

John turns, takes a deep breath, then walks to the courtroom door where Sarah is perched on a bench near the exit. She is unable to contain her feelings and lets a small laugh escape. John gives her a squinty eyed look and exits. Sarah follows closely behind him.

"So, Mr. Hot Shot Corporate Attorney, did I hear that you need to come back to receive punishment for your repeated tardiness?" she snickers again.

"Oh, I see you find this entertaining," John looks at her with a questioning face and slight smile.

"Maybe just a bit," she is extremely satisfied.

They walk to the clerk's desk where John requests a time slot to see the Judge. The elderly woman examines her computer to view the Judge's schedule, as Sarah hands a piece of paper to another clerk and is handed a folder.

"I have a case, shortly," Sarah announces, "and it looks like you will be hanging out for a while. Care to see how the pros do it?" she teases.

"Ohhh, the pros! Yes. And that would be you? Cute, Sarah," he takes a paper that the clerk hands him and looks at it. "Sure. I guess I will take you up on that since it looks like I have time to kill. And in what courtroom will this special performance take place where I might learn from a true professional?"

"Follow me kind Sir," Sarah curtsies. John rolls his eyes, and fights off a smile. They walk back to the elevator where they enter and ride to the next floor.

The door opens and they enter the hall where Sarah spots her client, a man who appears young enough to still be in high school. She speaks with him and escorts him into the courtroom where they take a seat on the benches. Sarah's case is quickly called in front of the Judge.

As she stands at the front of the courtroom, pleading her client's case, John sits in the back watching her with interest. A series of discussions go back and forth, ending with Sarah walking from the room with her client. As she passes John, she dramatically wipes her hand across her brow as if wiping sweat, in a motion of relief. John smiles and follows her out.

"Success. Congratulations," he says.

"No sarcasm?" she asks.

"No. I have to say that you did a good job and I must simply admit it and congratulate you. You got the results you were looking for, right?" he asks.

"Yes, I did, thank you," she answers as they walk back to the clerk's desk where Sarah hands over a stack of papers. Her client is close behind. She turns around and shakes his hand and tells him that he is free to go and instructs him as to what is required as a follow up. He thanks her and leaves.

Sarah turns to John, "I guess you have to get back to see Judge Conner?"

"Yeah. This should be interesting. Judge Conner must be having a bad day. I've never seen him like this," John adds.

"Maybe he is just tired of your cavalier attitude and tardiness," she responds.

"Cavalier?!" John defends. "Me? Cavalier? I don't think so. True, I have been late maybe a few times, but I hardly think that I have an attitude! And I hardly think it deserves penance."

"See? Cavalier! We aren't in New York anymore, Wonder Boy." Sarah is thoroughly enjoying the moment. "Well, if you don't mind, I am curious myself to hear what punishment he is going to bestow on you. May I?" she says motioning toward the elevator.

"If it would entertain you my lady, then of course," he says sarcastically. They take the elevator back up to the floor where Judge Conner presides. The two quietly enter the courtroom where Sarah positions herself in the front row to make sure that she doesn't miss a word. John scoots in next to her, waiting to be called. John looks closely at Sarah. "You are really enjoying this, aren't you?"

"No! Of course not," she defends, then smiles. "Oh, O.K., yes I am."

The Judge motions the bailiff over and whispers a few words. The bailiff nods his head and calls John to the bench.

"Whoa," John says leaning over to Sarah, "I thought that I'd be meeting in private."

"I guess not," she gives him a look of satisfaction that she will be able to enjoy the show.

"Mr. Rivera?" Judge Conner says, "Please join me up here at the bench." He pats the wooden counter where he usually strikes his gavel.

"Yes, your Honor," John stands and approaches the Judge.

"Mr. Rivera, I am going to get right to the point. Because you don't seem to value others time, I have decided to put *your* time to valuable use. Perhaps you will understand how important it is when it's taken from you. However, we are going to dedicate it to *good* use. This week, I saw an old friend, Mr. Landis. Mr. Landis is a local resident who places a Christmas tree on the top of his roof every year and every year he ends up in this courtroom. He violates building codes and refuses to remove it or change the placement," Judge Conner announces.

"Your Honor, I am aware of this case. I was in the courtroom recently when Mr. Landis appeared in front of you," he reveals.

"I see. Then you know that Mr. Landis is a harmless, although misdirected man. As much as his appearance has become a Christmas tradition around here, I always hope that one year he won't show up. But, again, he has been brought in for a violation that is costly and some times includes jail time. I don't want to see Mr. Landis go to jail, especially at Christmas time, do you?"

"Well, no your Honor, I don't," John says looking a little confused at where this speech is going.

"Seeing as though he is harmless, but determined, I can't help but think that there must be a solution to this matter. I can't imagine what it is, but I think that with some real effort, this problem can be resolved. Therefore, I am putting you in charge of finding that solution, Mr. Rivera," the Judge states proudly.

"A solution?" John repeats.

"Yes, Mr. Rivera, a solution. One that assures that Mr. Landis will never step foot in this courtroom again, at least not for this particular problem. You must keep in mind that he does not want assistance from legal counsel, nor will he consider placing the tree in a reasonable place on his property. The next time I see you, I want to hear that you found a solution that satisfies both the court's and Mr. Landis's requirements. If that means working weekends and nights, then that is what you will have to do. Although, we only have a couple of days until Christmas and I expect to have this resolved before that time because if you don't, he will be spending Christmas in jail."

"Your Honor, I am not exactly sure what it is I am supposed to accomplish. Short of suspending the tree by helicopter over the house, I don't know how we can resolve this," John respectfully responds.

"I think that might violate air space rules and regulations. I'm not sure. You may want to check on that one," Judge Conner gives him a sarcastic look. "See? You're already getting creative," he smiles. "And, Mr. Rivera, I am very aware of the circumstances surrounding the case better than anyone," he states, as he looks up to see Sarah sitting in the front bench who is looking smug and snickers.

"Ms. Wright!" Judge Conner barks out. Sarah looks up, wiping the smile off of her face. "As I recall, you have a special interest in this case and offered your services pro bono to Mr. Landis."

"Uh, yes, I did your Honor," she confirms.

The Judge continues. "Because your heart is in such matters, and because this is not going to be an easy problem to solve, I would like to assign you to the case to assist Mr. Rivera," he adds.

"Me?" she says totally surprised.

"Yes, Sarah, you," the Judge emphasizes. "He is going to need the help. You will both have to tolerate the situation and put your attention to something other than insulting one another. I believe that you can both learn a few things by working together on this. Perhaps you can do something good and bring a little Christmas cheer into the courtroom. Hmmm?" He pauses when he sees her taking a deep breath and sighs. "Is that a problem?" he asks.

"No! No your Honor. I would be happy to work on this case," she says as she sits up straight and puts on a happy face.

"Wonderful. Then you can go now." He looks at Sarah and then John. "Both of you." The two turn and slowly shuffle toward the exit until the Judge adds, "And I suggest that you start working on this immediately, because Christmas Eve is your official deadline," he smiles. "You are dismissed." They both remain frozen for a moment.

John stops and turns around, "Your Honor."

"Yes, Counselor Rivera? You had a question?" The Judge peers over his reading glasses.

"No, your Honor. Thank you, your Honor." John turns back to the exit door, looks at Sarah, rolls his eyes, and leaves, saying nothing. Sarah follows closely behind him.

As soon as they are safely out the doors and in the hallway, they burst out laughing.

"Are you kidding me?" John says smacking his forehead with his palm. "What kind of penance is that? This is crazy! I don't have time to eat, much less take on an impossible *do-gooder* project," he complains.

"I did offer to help Mr. Landis, but this is *really* unexpected. And we only have two days! I was happy to defend him, but I have no idea how we are going to find a *solution* to a tree on a roof, do you? He's been doing this for over 15 years! Plus, defending someone versus solving the actual problem ourselves. There is a big difference," she points out.

"Sarah, your guess is as good as mine. This is more up your alley," John answers.

"My alley? How in the heck am I supposed to know how to solve this? And, what does *my alley* mean anyway?" she stares at him, standing with her hands on her hips.

"You know. This fuzzy, warm, *help the poor schlep at Christmas time* kind of case. Unless he was eating the tree, it was toxic, and my client manufactured it, then don't look at me!" he quips back.

"Well, by golly, let's just make sure that doesn't happen, shall we?" she says overly sarcastic. "Let's get serious, John. This isn't helping. We know that he doesn't want anyone's help for starters, so working with him to find answers is out of the question. If we offer the obvious — moving the tree to another location — then we haven't really solved the problem the way I think Judge Conner is asking us to do. Mr. Landis won't comply anyway. So, I suggest that we start with research, don't you?" she adds.

"Sure. I guess. What are you thinking? We suspend it in a hot air balloon over the house? Hey, how about a hologram?" he says acting half serious.

"Actually, that isn't a bad idea. But, I think we need to go back to our roots," she adds.

"Our roots?" John asks.

"Yes, back to study hall — the law library at the University. It contains everything we could possibly need or want. We need to consider every possible option and that is going to take research. *Lots* of research! Are you available tomorrow?" she asks.

"Yeah, I think I can break away. I mean, this is going to cut into my case study time, but I can swing it," he agrees.

"I think this is going to take some real dedication on our part. Two days, John! Be sure to pack a thermos and bring a pillow. We're going to be there all night. I'll meet you on the library steps at 9:00 a.m., OK?"

"You've got it," he says and begins to walk down the hall then turns and yells, "And bring that positive 'miracles can happen' cornball Christmas spirit of yours. We're going to need it!"

"I'll do my best. I'll bring that and some sandwiches," Sarah laughs. She watches John enter the elevator and turns the opposite direction, heading for the clerk's office.

"Hey Margie," Sarah says to a kindly looking, elderly woman busily plucking at her computer.

"Miss Wright, hello. What can I do for you this fine day?' she asks.

"There is a Mr. Landis whose case I will be working on. May I see his file?" she politely asks.

"Sure. Just give me a moment. I believe it hasn't even been filed yet." The woman begins to sort through a pile of folders sitting on a desk next to her. "Yep, here it is. Do you need to check it out?" she asks.

"Please. But, Margie, I really wanted to ask you a few questions." The woman hands the file to Sarah who begins to sort through the information.

"Sure Ms. Wright, how can I help?"

"Margie," Sarah looks at her inquisitively. "Is it true that Mr. Landis has no phone, no email or other contact information, no driver's license or car, and his house title is not in his name?"

"Oh, yes. Mr. Landis. He is a unique one, he is. Has no phone, no way to contact him other than mail or pigeon. He lives in a home that his Aunt owned and left for him. That would be Mrs. Yates. So, it's in the Trust name on her behalf. I suppose that is how he has been able to stay there. It was paid for. He seems to like it that way. Total anonymity," Margie comments.

Sarah stares at the papers. "I just needed to make sure," she says to herself.

"I'm sorry?" Margie asks, not quite hearing the comment.

"Mr. Landis. I just was double checking to make sure that I didn't miss anything," Sarah says, again, speaking to herself.

"There isn't much to miss, Sarah. He doesn't seem to have any friends or relatives in his life, nor does he own anything," Margie adds. "Except that Christmas tree he puts on his roof every year. Poor man," she shakes her head in sadness.

"That's all I needed, Margie," Sarah hands the file back to her. She packs up her belongings and leaves the courthouse.

## Chapter Twelve

# Revealing Research

John sits on the grand steps of the University law library, a stately, stone building with huge Cathedral style windows and heavy entry doors. He sits on a newspaper to keep dry. Puffs of steam from two tall, paper cups of piping hot coffee float and hang in the air. Sarah arrives and briskly walks from the parking lot to the steps, abruptly stopping at his feet.

John's face lights up when he sees her standing before him. "You're late. Your coffee is getting cold," John hands her a cup.

"Well, someone is changing his ways," she says, "You are early! I'm impressed." Sarah places her gloved hands around the sides of the cup, seeking warmth.

"Come on. Let's get to work," she orders as she extends her hand to him so that she can help him stand up. He shakes his legs as if they had lost circulation.

"Let's get to the task at hand, shall we Watson?" John picks up a leather carry bag and slings it over his shoulder.

"Absolutely, Holmes," she replies and then stops. "Hey, why am I Watson? Why can't I be Holmes?"

"Up the stairs you go," he pats her on her back as they climb the stairs. Sarah stops and turns around. "I want to be Holmes!"

"Get in there," John teases.

They enter the library through the two heavy, oak doors and immediately enter silence. Only echoes of books being placed on tables, a chair scraping on the oak floor, and an occasional page turn can be heard. On the main floor are rows of very long, thick, wooden study tables. Low lighting lamps are bolted onto them, creating soft golden globes of light on the worn wood. The ceiling soars two stories, as do the grand windows that cast soft dust filled light beams in the room. A slight smell of old paper and mold tinge the air. There is a dark, sophistication to the atmosphere as students sit silently with piles of books, deeply entrenched in their studies.

"I think we should start with the actual building codes, don't you?" Sarah says quietly.

"That sounds like a plan. I am not remotely familiar with building codes. Let's hit it," John agrees, stops and looks at her. "And that would be where?"

"We need to go to the 3$^{rd}$ floor and back into the deep catacombs." Sarah leads the way to the elevator. "Follow me."

"We are going to need a couple of these," John grabs two book carts sitting in front of the elevator doors as they step on. They reach the 3$^{rd}$ floor, take off their coats, and place them on the carts along with their satchels. "You tackle those aisles and I'll tackle these. Let's load up the carts, circle around and meet on the main study floor at 1100 hours," John says, pointing and ordering.

"Right," Sarah responds as if taking orders from a drill sergeant then looks back at him with a questioning face.

"That would be eleven o'clock," John adds.

"I knew that!" she whispers and nods, pushing her cart toward her assigned section. She looks back at him and puts her hand up to her mouth and bites a finger nail, giving a 'dumb blond' look, making him chuckle.

They diligently seek any information that could give a clue to solving the bizarre problem. Any article, any book, rule or regulation finds its way on their carts. Could the solution be a cardboard or plastic imitation of a tree? Or lights without a tree? Why did it have to be an actual Christmas tree? And why on the roof? Thoughts and questions flood their minds. They continue to scour the aisles, carefully going through stacks and stacks of books.

Sarah sits on the floor with a stack of books next to her, fanning through pages, occassionally throwing one on her cart. Eventually, books overflow and begin to slide off when John appears in the aisle and removes a pile which he stacks onto a fresh cart. "Oh, thanks," Sarah responds, "I think we're going to be here a while. We're going to need a lot more coffee, don't you think?"

"I'm on the case," John smiles and reveals a thermos stashed inside of his jacket. "Let's roll these down to the first floor, park ourselves in a comfortable section where you can get started, and I'll replenish our coffee supply," he winks and turns to head for the elevator. "I'll leave my cart by the elevator on the first floor and meet up with you," he gives her a cute, childlike wave of his hand as the doors close.

Sarah laughs and shakes her head. She piles a few more books on the already large collection and heads to the first floor. As she arrives, she looks around the room, seeking a cozy corner and pushes her cart to a low, wooden table surrounded by worn out couches where she unloads the stacks of books. She then walks back to the elevator and wheels John's cart over when he shows up, hiding two cups under his coat. They walk to the chosen study spot where he pulls them out, handing one to Sarah and blowing on his hand after it burns him.

"Ouch!" he whispers. "I hope you like cream." He pulls packets from his pocket and places them on the table. "And just in case," he places the thermos in his bag on the floor under the table to hide it, "I brought an extra stash."

"Perfect!" Sarah whispers, keeping the cup below the table as she dumps a sweetener in. "It's going to be a long day."

"Night," John corrects.

"What?"

"A long night. It's going to be a long night." John begins to thumb through numerous sections, taking note of potentially important passages, and separating anything that may possibly be of relevance.

They continue to scour and mark pages with paper markers. As they work, John glimpses up at Sarah. "So, Sarah, what in the heck do you like to do when you aren't holed up in a courtroom?"

"Well," she pauses, running her index finger through chapters in a thick, musty, old book. "I'm a runner," she shares.

"That's right. I remember that in school. You still running? Very good," he replies.

"Whenever I get the chance. It's a stress reliever," she adds.

"And?" he pushes for more.

"And astronomy. Any interest in what's out there?" Sarah gestures to the window.

"I think if I knew more about it, I could totally get into it," he shares.

"Is that so? Well, I suppose I would be willing to instruct you with a basic lesson or two. The first time you actually find something cool in the telescope, and get a really good look, it's pretty exciting," she pauses. "Well, actually, it's amazing." Sarah looks out the window.

John examines her face and smiles. "I *would* like that."

Sarah suddenly becomes aware of her surroundings and gets back to work. "I guess we'd better get back to the books," she pulls another book from the pile and thumbs through it. A few minutes pass when Sarah randomly announces, "I love to cook."

"Excuse me? Did I hear you say you love to cook?" John's mouth opens as if in amazement and he teasingly puts his hand up to his ear pretending to listen intently.

"Yes, you did," she says with a sheepish smile. "I *love* to cook."

"Well, that is *great*! Because I . . . *love to eat*," they both say at the same time and laugh, disturbing nearby students studying.

"Oops, sorry," Sarah whispers to a young woman who gives her an annoyed look. "*And*," Sarah leans closer to John, "I especially love making sushi."

"Sushi! Yes," he says patting his heart with his hand. "Heaven!"

"Do you like to cook?" she asks.

"You know, I do. My Mother taught me many family recipes," John says with a happy face.

"Really? What kind of dishes?"

"Spicy Columbian dishes that would light your hair on fire," he says. "You know, it's funny how food can create such great memories, you know?" he says as if Sarah could relate.

"Yeah, I do know what you mean. There is something comforting about food. Those great smells, especially when its Mom's cooking," Sarah smiles. "That is really nice that your Mom shared the family recipes with you," she says. "Is your Mother from Columbia?" she asks.

"Yep. My parents came straight from the *old* country." "It was quite an accomplishment, coming to the United States."

"That is pretty cool," Sarah says. "So, I guess that means that you speak fluent Spanish?"

"Of course. Actually, it's a way of survival if you want to make sure that you know what's being said about you!" He smiles sweetly and pauses. "You know, my parents worked very hard to get to the U.S. and to provide a decent life for us." He pauses again. "Let me restate that. My parents worked hard to get us here, but my *Mother* worked really hard to make a good life for us."

"You mentioned that they aren't together anymore?" Sarah asks, putting a book aside.

"My Dad left my Mother when I was very young. She raised us," he pauses. "It was a real struggle for her, living in New York with three children, no education, no family to support her, limited English, and one income. It wasn't an easy task. But, she managed. Somehow she did it."

Sarah looks at him with compassion. "What about your Father? Did you have any contact or support from him?" she asks.

"No. I have no contact with him even to this day. I am not sure I truly can forgive him for abandoning my Mother in a new country, with 3 children and offering no support," John becomes very serious. "He simply bailed. Everything she did, she did for us. We struggled. I mean truly struggled. Many times we were thankful to have a meal on the table," he said with humility.

Sarah looks down, almost in shame. John notices her look of deep contemplation. "What? What are you thinking? I hope you aren't feeling sorry for me!" he adds.

"Wow, I feel ashamed. For some reason, I thought that you came from a wealthy family."

John looks confused and laughs. "Wow, what would make you think that?"

"You were a *very* well dressed, well spoken guy from New York, going to a great school, top of his class, studying corporate law. I made assumptions about you. I thought, well, that you were a spoiled rich kid," she confessed.

"What? Me? Are you serious?" he says with a look of entertainment.

"Yes, I did. I really did. New York, rich kid, spoiled, maybe following in Dad's footsteps to become a high powered attorney," she says looking down.

John laughs out loud as others look at him and 'shhhsh' him. He contains himself. "Now *that* is funny. We have known each other how many years? And all of this time, you thought you had the scoop on me," he pauses, "not that I go around sharing my childhood trauma story with everyone. But, I can honestly say that everything you see is the result of a great and dedicated Mom. It wasn't easy, Sarah. I had to work very hard to put myself through school," he says humbly.

Sarah stares at him. "I can't believe that I was so wrong."

"Well, I am sorry to disappoint you," he responds.

"No disappointment. I am just surprised," she says.

"That makes two of us. Life is a surprise," he thumbs through more pages. "Well, I think that we need to hunker down here and find out how we can keep Mr. Landis in business this year. What have you found?" he asks, abruptly changing the subject.

"Nothing so far. There are a couple of things you may want to take a look at," she passes a couple of books over to him and points at sections.

They continue their work, as the hours pass. John pulls out the thermos periodically and pours more coffee for them. They read through rules and regulations, pointing out pages to each other on occasion. Sarah sneaks sandwiches to John and they scarf whatever they can to avoid not having to leave their research post.

"Hey, take a look at this," John interrupts suddenly. "I believe that I may have stumbled on something here! There may be a loophole around our little problem." He slides the book over to Sarah who begins to read through the pages.

John continues. "The problem is simply *how* he is placing it on the roof. It appears that Mr. Landis may be able to keep his tree on the roof, for whatever insane reason he insists on doing that. Look, here is a case where a department store built a platform and didn't fix the tree on it, but that does apply to commercial business and buildings. In order to comply with regulations for a residence, we would need to build a platform and then *pot* it! It's like placing a plant on a balcony or a deck. If we secure it, without hammering it onto the roof like he's been doing, make sure that the lights are secured properly and safely, it should comply. Read this!" he says getting even more excited.

"Oh my gosh. This is so simple. You are right. It can be done for a residence! We just need to design a proper platform. A 'deck' as you said. Then add a container that we can safely secure, pot the tree, and decorate it with electrical connections that adhere to safety codes! Of course, we'll need to get a permit to do all of this," Sarah adds.

"I have the feeling that a certain Judge will expedite that for us in time for Christmas, don't you?" John says.

"Yes, I do!" Sarah laughs. "I can't believe it!" she says so excited that she throws her arms around John's neck and kisses him on the lips. He is surprised and laughs at her reaction.

"Oh, I'm sorry. I just couldn't help it. You are awesome," Sarah says enthusiastically, looking a little embarrassed at her own reaction. She grabs the book and looks at him. John is still staring at her, in disbelief.

"I am just so excited!" she laughs.

"No, no!" John laughs, "I'm happy. I'm happy that we don't have to sit here another ten hours and I am especially happy that you are so happy. This is great!" He begins to pile books on the cart. "So, now what do we do?" he stands and looks at Sarah, not sure what comes next.

"Well, I guess we build a platform! We'll need wood, and tools, nails of course, and a means to create a holder for the pot," Sarah says with satisfaction.

"And a very *big* pot!" John adds.

"Yes! A *very* big pot and a live tree to plant in it! Let's make copies of these pages so that we adhere to the details of the build-out. We don't want Judge Conner sending us back to detention if we get this wrong," Sarah says.

John chuckles, "You mean send *me* back to detention. I thought that this is the sort of thing you love to do! And," he says raising his eyebrows, "would spending more time with me be so bad?"

She looks at him and smiles. "No. No it wouldn't, John. Gosh! I am *so* happy! John, Mr. Landis is going to get to keep his tree, Judge Conner will be proud of us, and *you* have finished your assignment!"

"Not totally finished," he adds. "We need to do a little design work and then I suspect we need to carve out time to build this thing, don't you think?"

"Oh yeah, you are right. Tomorrow is Christmas Eve and we need to pull everything together and get it done before Mr. Landis gets hauled into jail. We need to create the design and dimensions and then make a list of materials. Building this thing is not going to be easy. We don't have a lot of time," Sarah adds.

"This calls for a little celebration, don't you think?" John suggests.

"John, we need to get home and figure out how we are going to do this. We don't have time to celebrate just yet," she blurts.

"Sarah," John quietly says. She is not paying attention and continues to close books and pile more on the cart. "Sarah, look at me," he says, touching her arm. She looks up as if shocked out of a trance. "There is no harm in joining me for dinner. You do have to eat. We'll celebrate when we finish, but certainly you can break for dinner," he beckons. "Besides, we need to sketch this thing out and make a shopping list as you said. Let's put the time to good use. No one is going to issue a permit or sell building materials this late at night."

She gives him a long look. "You are right. O.K., let's go grab dinner."

"Great," he says "I have the perfect place. Come on. Let's pack up and head over." They clear up their papers and debris. "I'll make copies and we can head out."

"Look!" Sarah says, pointing to the window. Large snowflakes are falling in slow motion, sparkling like crystals as they float past the glow from street lamps. "It's beautiful!" she packs up her bag.

"Yes. It's beautiful," John smiles and pauses, looking at Sarah. He sees the little girl in her again and is in awe. "Hey, sit tight. I'll be right back." He runs to get the copies made while she continues to clean up their research piles. Upon his return he grabs her satchel and stuffs a copy of their findings into it, taking a copy for himself and putting it into his own bag. John grabs both of their satchels, then takes Sarah's arm and hooks it in his as he walks her out the door of the library and down the steps. She pulls closer to him and smiles, as they walk to her car.

"Let's drop these off," John says as he places the bags into her trunk. I'll bring the regulations and a notebook to sketch this." He pulls out the documents and places them in a folder. "Are you up for a short walk?"

"Yes, some fresh air would be great." Sarah takes a deep breath and opens her arms wide to the sky. "Gosh, it's beautiful out." It is dark except for the glow of street lamps and store fronts. Shoppers hustle making last minute purchases, as stores close and lock up their doors. After walking a couple of blocks, John stops in front of a small restaurant and bows. "My lady? This is the place. Shall we?" He extends his arm and they enter.

*Chapter Thirteen*

# Making a Plan

Tables covered with crisp, white cloths hold small holly center-pieces sprayed with glistening silver, that sparkle from lit candle centers. John asks for a table near the window. The hostess directs them to one where they seat themselves across from one another.

"I thought you'd like to watch the snow," he smiles. "I should say that *I* like to watch you watching the snow." Sarah gives him a look of embarrassment and a coy smile. "I think this calls for an Irish coffee, don't you think?" he says with a big smile.

"Ahhh, the Irish coffee. Yes, let's," Sarah agrees.

John motions for a waitress. "Two Irish coffees and menus, please," he requests.

"Coming right up," a young server responds.

The two take their coats off, and John hangs them up on a coat rack nearby. He comes back to the table, sits down and leans over. "We may have to make this a Christmas tradition," he says.

"I think we already have," she adds. "A dead battery, and now a long night solving a case. There must be a better way to earn a drink!"

Their drinks and menus arrive. They quickly order food and get situated with their documents.

"I'm glad that you talked me into this," she smiles affectionately. He smiles back. "John," Sarah hesitates, "What you said in the library . . . about your family. Well, all of those times you flew back to New York. That was one of the reasons that I thought you were wealthy," she says.

"What made you think that?" he asks.

"It's expensive. I was worrying about paying for my books, but you . . . you were catching flights home on weekends. And you always dressed so well. And the corporate law path. It just seemed like, well, like you had it easy," she says.

John nods, knowingly and looks out the window at the flakes falling. "I guess I can see where you might have gotten that impression. Let me shed some light on this." John takes a deep breath and pauses for what seemed like several minutes to Sarah. "My Mother got a job for me in New York in the designer sweat shop where she worked. The pay was pretty good and I was able to save up enough to go to college, at least initially. But, when I got into law school, she became ill and things became difficult for her, so I came back on weekends to help her. I would take care of her, study, and work as much as possible. I worked with the designers, creating marketing plans and sales online. Sometimes, I'd even work in the design offices helping them in whatever way I could. It was a great way to make money and be with my Mom so that I could take care of things for her to make sure everything was in order and she was getting the care that she needed."

"As for the flights, they aren't expensive if you have a brother who works for the airlines. I never paid for a flight. It was my brother's way of helping out since he wasn't able to be in New York to help care for her. So, he made sure I could make it back to New York. I wouldn't schedule Friday or Monday classes which gave me four days with her. It wasn't easy, but I was all she had."

"Wow," Sarah says in total surprise. "And the clothes and corporate law path?" she asks.

"Oh, yeah, the clothes," John laughs. "My Mother was a seamstress in the garment district. Like I said, she worked for a clothing manufacturer and helped the designers. My clothes were free which were mostly samples, prototypes or clothes that were no longer being used for displays. They were really nice to us and would often let me model them, and keep them. She would tailor them for me. Sometimes she simply made some for me with remnants. She was an incredibly talented seamstress. One of the best," he smiles. "She wanted me to look good. Besides, I couldn't afford to spend money on clothes. Like you, I had books to buy."

"That is amazing," Sarah says quietly.

"Yes, she was something, my Mom. A hard working lady. It wasn't easy to watch her health decline. As for the corporate law," he pauses. "Sarah, if there was anything that I was determined to do, it was to give my Mother the life she deserved. I knew that if I worked hard enough and found a profession that paid well, I could support her in the kind of life style that my Father should have given her. There were so many years she spent in the sweat shops, sewing, and working to feed us kids. I wanted to get her out of there and finally, I managed to do that. Defending the poor wasn't going to pay her bills or mine," he says stating a fact.

"Wow, John. Your Mother must be extremely proud," she says with a kind and caring tone.

"Yeah," he smiles. "I think she was," he responds.

"Was?" Sarah asks.

"Yes, she died last year. That is why I left New York. I stayed with her until she passed away and once she was gone, there was nothing keeping me there. Then I got the offer here," John says. "I know you think it's crazy, but I always liked it here. I never would have left if it weren't for the circumstances and responsibilities of my family."

"Oh John, I am so sorry," Sarah says, tears welling in her eyes.

"I started making enough at my law practice to give her the proper medical attention she needed. The best care, in fact. Before she became totally bed ridden and would occasionally go into remission, I spoiled her with luxuries like a trip to Hawaii, and back to Columbia to visit her family. She was able to really enjoy her life without stress before we lost her. She deserved the best. My career, my income, allowed me to give that to her. I bought her a nice apartment in a safe area of New York, sent her to the best doctors, and got her in-home care right up until the end. I have no regrets," he responds. "I guess that's a long way around answering your question 'why corporate law?'"

Sarah is speechless. "You did an incredible thing. I had no idea." Her voice begins to crack. "I feel so ashamed."

"Why?" he asks, surprised.

"Well, we never knew anything about one another and all that time you could have reached out to me as your friend. I could have been a support system for you and helped in some way. Isn't it strange that it took all of this time for us to know these things?"

"Oh, I don't know. I think it isn't until you get older and wiser that you realize that it's O.K. to be who you are without the shame of being different. More important, it feels good to no longer need the approval of others. I hate to admit it, but perhaps I didn't want you to know the ugly truth, that John Rivera is the son of immigrants who barely spoke English. A guy whose Father split and had to worry about getting a new pair of shoes much less a present under the Christmas tree. Heck, I can't remember ever having a tree for that matter. Those aren't memories that are easy to deal with, much less share with someone . . . anyone. Your family always seemed so close and normal," John opens up.

"Normal?" Sarah gives a small laugh. "What is normal? And what did you have to be ashamed about, John? You didn't do anything wrong. We can't help what we come from, but what you did for your Mother was wonderful. That is something to be proud of," Sarah smiles at him with renewed interest.

"So, what about you? Now that I have revealed my deep dark secrets," he inquires.

"Hmmm," Sarah responds, taking another sip of her Irish coffee. The appetizers arrive and are placed between them. Sarah and John poke at calamari with their forks. "It's tough to talk about myself after hearing that." She pauses and takes a few bites of food.

"My Dad studied law and I always thought that it would be really cool to follow in his steps," she says thoughtfully.

"Really? I didn't realize that your Father was an attorney," John says.

"Well, funny that you mention becoming wiser about what we come from and where we are going. My Father is a retired construction worker. First a basic worker, then a Foreman, and a Manager, but a construction guy nonetheless," she says.

"O.K.," John responds looking confused. "Did I miss something? Didn't you say that your Father studied law?"

"Yes, he *studied* law. Unfortunately, he never finished, which brings me to learning a few things about myself that seem to be transparent to others," she replies.

"Like?" John asks.

"Like Judge Conner, for instance. After college, my Father married my Mother and then went to law school. Half way through, she got pregnant with me." Sarah pauses and looks at John. "It was not planned, and quite a surprise to them both. Neither of my parents came from families with money. With the cost of school and having a child, it put a strain on them financially. My Mother could no longer work long hours to help put my Dad through school. One of my Father's friends, who worked in construction, offered my Dad a job hoping to help out. He took it." She looks intently at John, "He never went back. I suppose he had intentions to do so, but that never happened. He worked his entire life in construction."

"Oh," John says, waiting to see if that was the end of the story, "And?"

"And, I have a wonderful Mother and Father who support and love me. They are happy, but I think I feel a bit guilty, like I am the reason why he never realized his dream," she finishes.

"That is sort of ironic," John smiles.

"Ironic?" Sarah pauses.

"Your Father and I have quite a bit in common if you think about it. We had different circumstances, but we chose family responsibility first, no matter what sacrifice that meant."

"What?" Sarah doesn't get it.

"Well, I took a different career path to take care of my Mother and I never went back. Here I am, in Corporate Law. Your Dad left school to take care of his family responsibilities and ended up staying on that path, ending up in construction. We both chose to make money to take care of a woman we loved and support family."

"Holy cow," Sarah says. "I never thought of it that way, but you're right," she says shaking her head.

"No regrets on his part?" John asks.

"No. None. He tells me he is happy about his decisions and everything that has happened. I guess it was meant to be."

"I see. So, is that why you became an attorney? " he asks. "To fulfill his dream? To make up for what *you* feel that he gave up or lost?"

"Judge Conner asked that question. He knows my parents well. I think that he believes I somehow feel guilty or responsible," Sarah shares.

"And the answer was?"

"I guess there was probably an underlying desire to fulfill his original goals. Probably more than I would like to admit. Sure, I know it wasn't my fault, but knowing I was the reason why he ended up quitting. Well, it's not the happy story anyone wants to hear about the circumstances of entering this world."

"Oh Sarah. Wow," John says, shaking his head and smiling. "What I did for my Mom . . . it was just life happening. And when life happens, you make decisions. If she hadn't gotten sick, things would be different, of course. But, they weren't and they aren't. I am happy with the decisions I've made along the way. I gave her everything she deserved and that felt really, really good. I have no regrets! I am sure that your Father feels the same way. Look at you! He has a beautiful daughter and a great family life. You shouldn't feel guilty about that. I know that you don't approve, but things didn't turn out so badly for me, either."

Sarah stares at John in silence. Tears come to her eyes. "You know, my Dad said the same thing, John. You are really opening my eyes." She looks at him seriously. "It's like I am getting this for the first time. I have hung on to things that haven't mattered to anyone but me. What I've been hanging onto isn't real. It's all about the experiences that make us who we are. It's not about making 'wrong' decisions. I get it. I really do." John smiles and takes her hand in his. Sarah continues. "I've been so hung up on ridged ideas about how things 'should be' instead of how things are, that I've lost the whole point of life. It's the journey, and allowing it to take you where you need to be." She looks off into the distance and shakes her head as if she just woke up. "You know, maybe that is why I am so intent on making a difference." She looks at John seriously.

"Maybe," he squeezes her hand. "But, that isn't such a bad thing." He kisses her hand. "I think that you are pretty great, no matter what motivates you. You believe in miracles. I like that," he states nodding his head in approval.

"And you? Have your struggles killed off your ability to believe in miracles?" Sarah questions him.

John thinks long before replying. "I don't know. I think that the day my Father left, I stopped believing in anything. I was focused on surviving. There were no miracles in my life and Christmas, well, there were no miracles at Christmas. I am not sure I believe in them. Perhaps you are right."

"I am so sorry, John. I am sorry about the loss of your Father, the loss of your Mother, for judging you. I know that I have my own baggage, but I still believe in miracles. Isn't there anything I can do to renew your faith in the possibilities?"

"Sarah, you have enough faith for the both of us. I will contribute to your causes as much as I can, but I can't promise you that I will share your enthusiasm. And I believe that we have a task at hand with our Mr. Landis. *That* would be miracle enough for me!"

Sarah laughs, "O.K. That's a deal. Let's get to it."

John pulls out a pen. "I have an idea," he sketches wildly for a few minutes and turns the pad of paper around for Sarah to view. "Take a look at this," he waits for her to examine his design.

"I love it. I think that will work," she nods, taking the pen and adding a few strokes. "What if we added this?" She turns the drawing around for John to view, who nods in approval.

"We'd better make a list of materials," he pulls the pad of paper back toward him and writes down items. "Let's finish dinner and get home so that we can tackle this early."

They continue to scribble on their notebook, eat and drink. The table candles twinkle and burn low as they continue to work. Random snowflakes silently fall outside the window.

## Chapter Fourteen
# Up on a Roof

Sarah sits in a tiny coffee shop, where she has secured two seats at a small table top, waiting for John to arrive. Two small plates, each with a slice of Pumpkin bread are on the table. She looks out of the shop window, nervously tapping her toe. Suddenly, John appears at the entrance and looks in the glass window. He wipes off a circle of mist, spots Sarah, gives her a wave then enters. He looks handsome, in jeans that show off his fit physique, a thick plaid shirt, and scarf. He is unshaven and looks ruggedly sexy. As he approaches Sarah's table, he pulls a piece of paper out of his pocket and waves it in front of her. "You might be interested to see what I picked up this morning, complements of Judge Conner."

"No! Is that our building permit? How did you pull that off?" Sarah exclaims.

John gives a big, proud smile. "I figured since we did such a good job at tackling this assignment that the Judge would be happy to facilitate our efforts. I called him late last night."

"Very resourceful! I am impressed." Sarah pushes a plate toward him. "Pumpkin bread?"

"Absolutely," he takes a bite. "Thanks."

"You seem pretty chipper this morning. I'd say that someone is getting in the spirit of Christmas and giving," she winks at him.

"Yes, so let's get to it before I change my mind! Let me just grab a coffee to go and we'll head out. The truck is loaded with everything that we need. Do you want anything else?" he says motioning to the serving counter.

"No," Sarah looks at him with a big smile, "I believe that I have everything I need."

John gives her a sheepish grin and walks to the counter where he places his order and quickly returns to the table with his coffee. "Ready?" he asks. "I'll drive if you feed me Pumpkin bread."

"Deal," Sarah agrees.

They jump into John's truck parked just outside on the street and quickly drive away. The truck pulls in front of Mr. Landis's house, where John parks at the curb. The two get out and pause on the front lawn, examining the worn, sad house. On the roof sits a pole and several strands of Christmas lights that swing in the wind. On the lawn a tree lays on its side, strewn with icicles, torn from its foundation and tossed.

"It looks like someone took care of the violation," John comments, then walks to the front porch and knocks on the door. No one answers. He peeks in the window, but sees nothing. "No answer!" he yells back to Sarah. "I guess we should get started. Maybe he'll show." She nods and begins to unload the contents of the truck bed. John takes the permit out of his jacket and tacks it to the front porch. "That should hold us for now," he says aloud.

The pair gets busy unloading plywood, boards, a saw horse, various supplies, and a tool box. A very large pot remains in the truck. John takes the ladder that is propped on the side of the house and extends it to the roof. He returns to the front lawn where he sets up a saw horse and runs extension cords from the house. He plugs in a rotary saw, measures and begins to cut large sections of plywood and two by fours, handing pieces to Sarah who carts them to the base of the ladder.

"Sarah, how are you with heights?" John points to the roof.

"I can handle it," she answers.

"I just need you to mark off where the platform will go and take a few other measurements for me. Are you up for it?" he asks.

"Absolutely," Sarah spryly jogs to the ladder and pops up it, carefully navigating the roof top, measuring and writing down her results. John watches her and nods his head in approval of her confidence. She carefully climbs down the ladder, walks to where John continues to measure and cut wood, and hands him the results. They continue to work, occasionally sipping coffee, and carting materials up the ladder. The two eventually end up on the roof, hammering and building a platform with their materials, working as if experienced contractors. Hours go by as they diligently hammer and build.

It is getting late in the day as they secure the final pieces of the platform. "I think this is it," John says. "It's time to get the tree up here, but we have to get that pot secured first. That is going to be a challenge, but I have some ideas," he shares with Sarah.

"John, let's climb down," Sarah suggests.

"Sure. Do you have an idea?" he asks.

"Let's climb down and I'll tell you when we get down there," she says.

"O.K." John is curious.

"Trust me," Sarah touches his arm and pulls him toward the ladder where they climb to the bottom.

"O.K., mystery woman. I guess you have a plan," John gives in.

"That I do. You aren't the only one who spoke to Judge Conner," she says as she dusts herself off. "He told me that he would be coming by to check on our work. So, we need to hold off on putting the tree up there. He wants to make sure that we are adhering to building codes, since he pulled strings for us," she shares. "We've been working pretty hard. Let's take a break."

"I am starving. Let's order a pizza. First, let me put the extension cords in place. And," he says excitedly, "I brought something special for the occasion." He walks over to his tool kit and pulls out a timer. "Take a look at this," he smiles and walks to the side of the house where he plugs it in and sets it. He connects the extension cord and walks back to Sarah. "Mr. Landis's Christmas will come on and off at the appropriate times!"

"Perfect," Sarah laughs and turns when she hears someone yelling. Waving from across the street and walking toward her are her parents, bundled in coats. Her Father is carrying a large basket. "Hi there!" Sarah shouts. They reach the front lawn and hug her. Sarah's Father hands her the basket which she almost drops, not realizing how heavy it is. "Whoa! What's in here?" she peeks under the cloth draped over the top.

"We saw you two kids working hard all day. I don't want to be nosey, but I know that you haven't stopped to eat, so we wanted to bring over some food, and drinks," her Mother responds, looking at her Father as they both smile in agreement.

"Mrs. Wright, this is *really* nice! Thank you," John looks at the hot ham and cheese sandwiches wrapped in foil, cheesecake, steaming crab cakes, and hot cider. "Did you make all of this?"

"Yes, I did. But first, John, come over here," Sarah's Mom opens her arms and waves him over. John walks to her and she gives him a big hug. "It is so wonderful to see you again! You did such a great job at the tree lighting, playing Santa," she says. "Are you hungry?"

"Mrs. Wright, it's great to see you both again. And, yes, I am starving," he says as he pulls out the contents of the basket.

"There are plates and silverware in there. Just throw it all back in the basket and drop it off on your way out," Sarah's Mom explains.

Sarah's Father shakes John's hand, "It's really nice to see you John. This is really nice, what you are doing for Mr. Landis," he says.

"Well, Mr. Wright, I can't really take credit for doing a good deed. I was actually ordered by Judge Conner to work on this. Your daughter, on the other hand, is assisting as a favor to me and Judge Conner. So, she really gets the credit for doing the good deed. I couldn't have done this on my own," he shares.

"John found the solution, Dad. Then he designed the platform. Isn't that great?" she says proudly.

"That *is* great, John. I am sure that you will make a very sad man very happy this holiday season. The authorities yanked the tree off last night. It would have broken his heart not to have it back up by

Christmas. Imagine how he will feel when he comes home to find his tree on his roof, looking better than ever, complements of local, caring people. You are doing a really nice thing," Sarah's Dad states, nodding his head in approval.

"Well, we haven't seen Mr. Landis so far today, but I am sure it will be a nice surprise once he shows up. I hate to admit that it didn't start out to be a good deed on my part, but it is feeling pretty good now," John says as he looks at Sarah and smiles. "Of course, I am in great company." She smiles back.

"Mom, this is incredible. Thank you so much!" Sarah says, filling her plate with the beautifully packaged foods. She grabs her Mother and gives her a strong hug.

"Oh gosh, Sarah, I am happy to do it. Look, we don't want to interrupt," Mom continues. "We just wanted to run over here and say 'hello' and drop off the food. John, are you spending time with your family Christmas Eve?" Sarah gives her a wide eyed stare as she takes a big bite of a sandwich.

"No, Mrs. Wright," he responds.

"Oh, you aren't going back to New York?" she asks.

"My Mother passed away a year ago, Mrs. Wright," he shares.

"Oh no, John. I am so sorry to hear that. Come here," she says, steps forward and gives him another hug. "Why don't you spend Christmas Eve with us? It would mean so much to Jim and I, and I am sure Sarah would love it." Her Mother looks over at Sarah with a clever look.

John looks at Sarah who is still staring at her Mother. "Oh no, Mrs. Wright, I couldn't impose," he responds.

"Sure you could! Besides, you aren't imposing. Everyone is welcome, including our neighbor, Mrs. Costello," she waves at Mrs. Costello's window where she sits watching. "It would be so wonderful if you joined us. Please say that you will," she pauses. "Unless you have plans already, of course," she adds.

"No, I don't, actually, and I would love to," he says carefully examining Sarah's face. She smiles at him, nervously. "May I bring anything?" he offers.

"Not a thing. Sarah, your Father will make his usual overly spiked eggnog. John, you've been warned. We'll see you at 7:00 p.m. tomorrow night then?" she asks.

"It will be my pleasure," he shakes Mr. Wright's hand again.

"Your Father and I are going to leave you two to finish your work here. Make sure that you are well rested for the holiday celebration tomorrow," she says as she turns away and smiles to herself, making sure that Sarah doesn't see her. She and Sarah's Father walk back to their home.

Mr. Wright turns around and shouts, "We can't wait to see the tree back up! Good work!"

"Your parents sure are nice, Sarah," John says.

"Yeah, they are great," Sarah agrees as they unpack more food from the basket. John walks over to his truck and starts it, cranking up the blowers to create heat. They climb inside and balance their plates on their laps.

"So Sarah," John says taking a bite of crab cake. "I have a question."

"Sure," she responds.

"Do you think that maybe you haven't gotten close to anyone because you think that it might interfere with your career plans?"

"What?" Sarah responds, looking confused. "Where did that come from?"

"Well, it looked painful for you to have me join you tomorrow. It got me to thinking. Your Dad was all set to become a lawyer, got married, had you, and the course of his life changed. Do you think that maybe somewhere in your mind, you are afraid to get close to anyone because you think it will control you or mess up your career plans? You know, fall in love and do something radical like get married or worse, have a child?"

"Of course not," she responds.

"No?" he says. "Are you sure? You know, love makes people do strange things. If you fell in love, you could lose control," John shares. Sarah continues to eat in silence. John continues. "Sarah, I think that you are determined not to let a relationship get in the way of your aspirations," he adds.

"What? Don't be silly," Sarah says.

"Well, if you got close to someone, would it be so bad?" he asks.

"John, no. That is not it," Sarah defends. John gives her a sarcastic look of disbelief. "OK, maybe I am a bit protective. I am just into my career, John. It's not personal," she defends.

"Sarah, you wonder why you don't know anything about me after so many years. Well, besides my pride, a lot of it's because you never allowed me to get close. I think having feelings for someone petrifies you and you think it makes you vulnerable. You became an attorney to follow your Dad's path, only this time you won't let anyone get in the way of that path or make the same mistakes," he adds.

"John, I can see how you would think that, but no, it's just not the case," she defends. Just then, Judge Conner pulls in front of the house. They look at each other and the conversation stops. They place their plates and cups back in the basket and walk over to greet the Judge.

"Judge Conner," John shouts. "It is great to see you. Thank you for coming by on Christmas Eve. We're ready for you."

"Wonderful!" the Judge says. "I have to say that I am impressed at how quickly you resolved this issue. Just in time for Christmas. Now let's get up on that roof and take a look."

The Judge joins John as they walk to the side of the house, where they climb the ladder to the roof top. Portly Judge Conner struggles but confidently makes his way to the top where they examine the platform. The Judge points at spots, pulls at corners, and jumps up and down on the platform. They continue to examine the work until Judge Conner shakes John's hand and after a few minutes climb back down.

"Good job, Sarah," the Judge says as they walk back to the front lawn where she is standing. "You two make a great team," he smiles as John walks up behind him.

"I think so," John adds, looking fondly at Sarah.

"I think that the platform is ready for the final addition," John announces. "This is going to be the tough part, so I am glad you are here, Judge Conner. We need to get that very big pot up there and secure it before we can hoist the tree up. Any chance that we can enlist your assistance? I have a plan to wench it up."

"Absolutely," Judge Conner adds. "Actually, that should be happening right about now," he says as he looks at his watch.

"I'm sorry?" John asks, confused at the comment. The Judge looks at his watch again and looks in the sky. Suddenly they hear a whooshing noise like a large vacillating fan. The noise continues to get louder until they can see a helicopter nearing their location. They all look up as it gets closer to where they are standing. Sarah and John are squinting, trying to see what it is doing and become nervous at how close the helicopter is flying.

"What is that helicopter doing here?" John looks at Judge Conner trying to figure out what its purpose might be. The Judge seems totally unsurprised and watches the sky intently. He looks at John and points up. As it nears, they can see that there is a large object hanging from the bottom by a rope. The helicopter nears and hovers. Finally, they see that the large object dangling is a Christmas tree in a pot, contained in a large, thick net. It swings back and forth as the helicopter positions itself.

"I think it's time to get back up on that roof, John," the Judge says. "Care to join me?" The Judge waves to the helicopter.

"No way," John says, with his mouth open. "No way!" The Judge walks to the ladder. John turns to Sarah. "I knew he was wealthy, but this is unbelievable!"

"John? Are you coming?" The Judge asks, smirking at their reaction.

"Yes! Coming," John responds as he jogs over to the ladder and climbs up after the Judge. He looks back at Sarah and shrugs his shoulders and shakes his head.

"He wasn't kidding when he said he had a surprise for us," Sarah says to herself as the two men climb to the roof. "Holy Toledo!" she says barely able to hear herself above the helicopter engine and swooshing of blades.

John and Judge Conner secure themselves against the platform. The tree is slowly dropped down as the helicopter hovers and lowers the rope while the men carefully guide the tree. Hearing the noise, neighbors gather on the front lawn, including Sarah's parents. All are looking and pointing, gasping in amazement at the spectacle.

The men guide the tree in place, and motion for the helicopter to release the rope. The net releases, leaving the tree solidly in place, as they guide the rope to make sure that it does not swing and hit them. The helicopter hovers as Judge Conner gives the pilot a salute and wave. The neighbors on the lawn all begin to applaud.

"This is one heck of a show!" Mr. Wright exclaims as they join Sarah on the front lawn of the Landis house.

"Oh my gosh, Dad, Mom. Look! It's already decorated!" she shouts with excitement. "It's beautiful!"

"Sarah!" John yells as he plugs the tree into the extension cord secured on the roof. "Do us the honors!" By now an even bigger crowd has gathered, laughing and cheering in excitement. The sky is grey and darkness has set in.

Sarah walks over to the extension cord and looks around at the people now packed on the front lawn and along the sidewalk. "Are you ready?" They all yell in excitement and encourage her, clapping their hands. Sarah plugs the cord into the house electrical box and the tree lights up, looking magnificent and brilliant.

John jumps up and down on the roof, arms over his head in triumph and whoops out loud. The audience now applauds and yells, laughing and pointing at the beautiful display. Judge Conner gives John a high five and they wave at the audience below and climb down the ladder. The crowd continues to clap, laughing and hugging one another.

Judge Conner shakes hands with everyone as he moves through the crowd, many patting him on the back in congratulations. The Judge turns to Sarah and John, "John, go ahead and secure it with bolts and then make sure that Mr. Landis comes back into the courtroom right after Christmas. Please speak with him, both of you, and make sure he knows that it is simply a follow up visit so that he understands what transpired and what is expected in the future. He can leave the platform and container. But, he must dispose of all of the old trees and any others he puts up in the future. The structure must remain secure, of course."

"Your Honor, I am happy to take the dead trees away," John says gesturing to the stack of dried out trees on the side of the house. "I have room in my truck and can dispose of them properly. I'll load them up before we leave," John offers.

"Thank you, John. Speaking of Mr. Landis, have you seen him today?" the Judge asks.

"No, Judge Conner. He doesn't appear to be home. Perhaps he thought we were going to take his tree away or take him to jail," Sarah says.

"Well, let's make sure that we never see him in our courtroom for this offense again." The Judge looks around at the smiling neighbors. "I think you've found a solution that has made everyone happy. One that I am sure he will be very excited and surprised to see upon his return to the house," he smiles.

"I think so, your Honor," John adds.

"Joe," the Judge says. "Outside of the courtroom, you can simply call me Joe."

"Thanks, your, uh Joe," John laughs and shakes his hand. "That was one heck of an entrance!"

"Well, it wouldn't be fun to die with a pile of money when you can do something good with it . . . something fun!" the Judge smiles. "And John, you two have impressed me. I have to be honest. I didn't think that you could pull this off. What you did here is a tribute to your tenacity and your spirit." The Judge gives John a strong hand shake and hugs Sarah.

"I think I'll go visit with your parents, Sarah. We have a lot of catching up to do," he adds and crosses the street to catch up with Mr. and Mrs. Wright. They begin to laugh and loudly speak over one another. The three friends continue to chat as they walk to the Wright house and disappear inside.

A group of carolers is walking down the street and stops in front of the Landis house. They gasp and point at the beautiful tree on the roof then resume their singing. The remaining neighbors who had collected on the lawn begin to join them in singing carols and then disband, happily discussing the exciting event.

John drags the dead trees piled on the side of the house across the front lawn and loads them into his truck bed. Sarah collects tools and equipment, placing everything in John's truck.

"Shall we wait a bit to see if Mr. Landis shows?" Sarah asks.

"I suppose we could hang around a little longer. Come on," John says. "I still need to bolt the pot onto the platform. Plus, I have a little surprise for us." He goes into the back of the truck and pulls a bag out of a cooler. "Join me," he says, putting his hand out for her to take. She looks at it, hesitates, and takes his hand.

"Where are we going?" Sarah asks.

"Back on the roof, my dear, back on the roof," he crooks his finger, luring her.

"Wait!" Sarah has a look of excitement and runs to the truck. She grabs a big carry bag and starts to rifle through it. "I think I know what I'm supposed to do with this," she says pulling out the dazzling star that Judge Conner, or whoever that mysterious figure was, gave her.

"Oh, the magical star. It's perfect. Come on." He swings his pack on his back and they walk to the side of the house where he helps her up the ladder, climbing closely behind her to make sure she does not fall. Once they reach the top, they situate themselves on the platform, sitting next to the dazzling, lit tree. It is totally dark, and the tree is ablaze with color.

John tightens several bolts before pulling his back pack near to him. "Are you ready?" he asks.

"Ready for what?" Sarah asks.

"For this," John pulls out a bottle of champagne and two glasses.

Sarah gasps. "You didn't! That is so sweet!"

"Well, I thought this called for a little celebration, don't you? I think we finally earned it," he places the bottle on the platform.

"Yes, I certainly do," she giggles. John pops the cork and pours two glasses.

"Wait!" she says putting her glass down on the platform. She steps over to the tree and places the star on the top. It glitters and the light from it intensifies. Sarah takes her seat next to John again.

John turns to Sarah, "Is that the star Judge Conner gave you?"

"Judge Conner, Father Christmas, or maybe an angel," she raises her eyebrows.

"Father Christmas or an angel?" John looks at her confused.

"I'll tell you some other time. It is amazing. This is where it belongs, don't you think?" She stares at its brilliance.

"Yes. This is where it belongs," he smiles at her and raises his glass. "A toast!"

"Yes, a toast," Sarah lifts her glass into the air.

"You were right," John says.

"About what?" Sarah asks.

"About the tree. It's pretty cool. I like it. I mean I like doing something special, even if it seems kooky," he says staring at it.

"Here's to doing something nice, no matter how crazy it might seem," she gives him a big smile, looking up at the tree. "Yeah, it is pretty cool. It feels good and it feels right. Crazy, but right." He pours more champagne in their glasses.

"Yep, it feels pretty good," he agrees and shakes his head, as he stares at the tree. "So, did you ever think you'd be celebrating Christmas on a rooftop, with a Christmas tree no less?"

"It is pretty unique, that's for sure. We have one heck of a view up here, though," she looks up at the crystal clear sky and stars above.

"Yes, the view sure is great," John says staring at Sarah. "Well, we did it Counselor Wright," he smiles.

"We certainly did, and in a very dramatic way!" she laughs.

John looks at her with a serious look. "We make a good team, don't you think?"

She clinks his glass. "Yes, we do," she agrees, taking a sip.

They are silent for a few minutes, taking in the beauty of the sky, the sparkling, bright tree, and the incredible rooftop view. "It doesn't look like our Mr. Landis is going to show up," John notes, looking down at the driveway below.

"No, it doesn't. I'd like to see his face when he sees this, though. I'll bet it's the last thing he thought we'd be doing . . . putting his tree back up on his roof," Sarah raises an eyebrow.

"I am sure it is," John agrees.

They continue to drink their champagne and stare at the sky and tree, leaning back on the roof like little kids who are star gazing on a front lawn.

"John," Sarah begins, "You are right."

"Hmm? About what?" he asks.

"About not getting close to anyone. I never wanted to admit it. I'm 33 years old and I have never let a man get close to me. I guess I always thought that falling in love might mean compromising my dreams," she says looking at him seriously. "The whole story about my Dad, and what you said, well, I think you are right. I don't want to commit to share in anyone else's life for fear of losing mine."

"Sarah, what are your dreams?" John asks.

"My dreams?" Sarah pauses to think. "Gosh, I guess being able to pursue my career, taking care of scrappy, unwanted animals, having good and loving people around me."

"I think that is a wonderful dream. I don't see why you can't have that and romance too," John takes her chin in his hand and turns her face toward him. "Don't you agree?"

"Yes. I do. It's funny how we get stuck in fear. You know?" Sarah looks sweetly into his eyes.

"Yes, I do know. Unfortunately, we all operate in fear on some level," he places his arm around her.

"As for your Father, I think he is one of the few people who didn't make a decision based on fear. He just allows life to flow and take him in wonderful directions, and he doesn't look back. Having you was a gift to him. Your parents, well, they are incredible. I never got to experience that – seeing parents so dedicated to one another, no matter what challenges they meet. That is real love. What a wonderful family you have. Celebrate it. What we did for Mr. Landis, and what you do for everyone you come in contact with whether it's the courtroom or daily life – that is giving from the heart. It's wonderful. You are wonderful, Sarah," he says touching her face lightly.

Tears are streaming down Sarah's face. She leans over and places a soft kiss on his lips. He kisses her back and they hold each other, and kiss passionately. Sarah pulls away and looks at him surprised at her spontaneity, and they both begin to laugh.

"That's a good start," John teases.

Sarah laughs. "John, I truly am looking forward to having you join us for Christmas Eve. I just wanted you to know that."

"Thanks," John says. "I am very much looking forward to it." They sit in the silent night, looking up at the stars and the sparkling tree, their arms around one another. The decorations light up the street down below. The tree top star flashes brightly.

## Chapter Fifteen
# A Miracle or Two

J ohn pulls into the Wright's driveway. He turns to look at the tree sparkling on the roof behind him, pauses and smiles. He steps onto the Wright porch and knocks on the door. The Wright's home cheerfully displays colorful Christmas lights. Sarah opens the door and greets him, throwing her arms around his neck. She is wearing a little black dress that shows off a slender, stunning figure. Her face is glowing.

"Wow," John gasps. "You look incredible!"

She smiles and grabs his hand, yanking him through the doorway. "Get in here! It's cold outside. Mom! Dad! John's here!" she shouts. Everyone cheers and greets him.

Doug and his girlfriend come out of the kitchen with food and drinks. Doug yells, "Dude! It's great to see you!" He slaps John's hand and shakes it hard. "I hear you are a hot shot attorney now!" he jokes.

"I try," John smiles. "I hear you are a hot shot entrepreneur."

"The best!" Doug teases. "The best!"

"And humble as ever," Sarah quips back, taking John's coat.

Mrs. Wright enters the room with a plate of appetizers and places it on the living room coffee table. "You made it! It is so good to see you, John. Make yourself comfortable and go help yourself to the food."

"Thank you, Mrs. Wright. I will. Thank you for having me," John responds politely.

"Hey there counselor, how about the famous Jim Wright egg-nog?!" Mr. Wright says, entering the room and handing him a glass.

"Careful! Careful! That is rocket fuel," Sarah's Mom warns him again.

"Thanks for the warning, Mrs. Wright. I will proceed with caution," John laughs.

Sarah and John pick at appetizers, toast to the season, and banter about football and other matters. The Wright's home is full of laughter and cheer. Sarah and John occasionally give one another affectionate glances as they visit with the family and friends who periodically join the party.

Sarah slips away and joins her Mom in the kitchen. She places her arm around her Mother and kisses her cheek.

"What is that for?" her Mother says with a surprised look.

"Just for being so wonderful," Sarah says with a serious look.

Her Mother laughs, "Well thank you, sweetheart! I love you, and we really love that John," she looks at Sarah sheepishly.

"I know Mom. I do too. I do too," she smiles.

"Here, take these into the living room and feed that husky brother of yours!" her Mother orders, handing her more appetizers. Sarah takes the plate and walks back into the living room, handing it to Doug and his girlfriend, Stephanie.

John walks to the living room window and looks out at the sparkling, lit tree on the roof across the street. Sarah walks up next to him.

"So, have we seen our Mr. Landis yet?" he asks.

"There are lights on in the house," Sarah says. "I believe he is in there."

John looks at her. "Perhaps it's time for that visit, don't you think?"

"I do," she agrees. "But hold on just a moment."

Sarah goes into the kitchen and comes back out with a bottle of champagne and three glasses. "I'm ready," she says putting on her coat.

They walk across the street, holding one another as they walk up the big front porch and to the door. John knocks. Mr. Landis carefully peeks out the window and opens the door.

"Mr. Landis," John begins, "I'm John Rivera and I believe you know your neighbor here, Sarah. We were the attorneys in charge of . . . "

"I know who you are," he says without emotion. Sarah and John are not sure what to think, nervous at what might come next. Mr. Landis stares at the floor, taking a long time to speak. "I am grateful for what you did. Very grateful," he says quietly and shyly. They both sigh in relief.

"It was our pleasure, Mr. Landis," Sarah adds. "We have a few things to wrap up next week, but there is no rush. I will arrange another meeting at the courthouse just to make sure that you under-stand all of the conditions. Basically, you are all set, provided that you dispose of the trees properly in the future and continue to secure the tree on the platform, in the same manner every year."

"That won't be a problem, Miss. I have my tree. For that I am forever grateful," he says again.

"In light of the outcome, we want to wish you a Merry Christmas and celebrate. Will you join us for a glass of champagne?' John asks.

"I don't usually drink, but sure. I am happy to share a glass of Christmas cheer," Mr. Landis replies. "Would you care to come in-side?" he asks. "It ain't fancy, but it's warm."

"Thank you," Sarah says, entering the house.

John unwraps the gold seal on the bottle as Sarah places the cham-pagne glasses on a coffee table in the living room. The home is simple, but clean. There are no Christmas decorations inside. It is dimly lit and the furniture is sparse, old and worn.

John pops the cork and Sarah cheers. He pours champagne into each of the glasses. They raise their glasses, ready for their toast.

"To Christmas miracles," John says, smiling at Sarah.

"To Christmas miracles," she responds. All three clink their glasses.

"Much obliged," Mr. Landis adds with a grateful look.

As they sip their champagne, headlights shine brightly into the living room. They look out the window to see a car pull into the Landis driveway, hopeful that the police have not returned.

"John," Sarah looks at John, worried that they must deal with an unhappy neighbor or law enforcement.

"Not to worry, Mr. Landis," John assures him. "We have the permit displayed and there should be no more issues. We posted it on the porch, so you only need to make sure that it stays there to avoid any more house calls."

Mr. Landis continues to stare at the car with strong interest. He places his glass down, walks to the door, and opens it, standing in the doorway. A young man gets out of the driver's side and walks to the front lawn. He stares up at the tree.

Sarah and John look at each other confused. They say nothing. Sarah shrugs her shoulders.

The young man, about 18 years of age, walks to the bottom of the porch and looks at Mr. Landis. His mouth begins to quiver and tears roll down his cheeks. "Dad?" he asks, "Dad?"

"David?" Mr. Landis starts crying as he nods his head. He opens his arms and the young man walks up the porch steps and collapses into them. They hug tightly. John and Sarah look at each other confused.

Sarah and John walk out onto the porch. The young man notices them after a few minutes of crying and hugging. "I'm sorry," Mr. Landis says, "This is my son, David. David, these are friends of mine. Good friends of mine."

The boy turns to them and shakes their hands. "I'm sorry, I apologize, but I haven't seen my Father since I was 3 years old." He looks at Mr. Landis who has his arm around him, tears still streaming down his face, and pauses. "You see my Mother took me away from this house. It was Christmas Eve and she left suddenly in a rage, packed all of our things and left for good. She told me that we would never see him again. But, before my Mother put me in the car, my Dad pulled me aside. He told me that no matter what, no matter how long, that if I ever wanted to find him, all I had to do was to find the house with the Christmas tree on the roof. That I would know for sure that it would be him. Every year that I could, I tried to find the tree. When I was old enough to drive, I would sneak away searching for the house with the tree. You see, my Mother was emotionally unstable and moved us constantly to other cities. She made it difficult, but, I never forgot, and I knew some day I'd find my Dad." He looks at his Father and continues. "Dad, I never forgot. I knew you wouldn't give up on me. I found the tree. I found it! I found you!" He sobs into his Father's shoulder as they hug tightly, both crying.

By now, Sarah has tears streaming down her cheeks. "All this time," she says looking at Mr. Landis in total awe, "the tree, on the roof?" He smiles and nods his head.

Sarah and John are amazed at what they are witnessing. The seemingly insane neighbor had diligently displayed a beacon for his lost son every year, regardless of the consequences. Tears stream down Sarah's cheeks, and John's eyes well up. They hug Mr. Landis and his son, all crying and then laughing.

Sarah wipes her tears. "Oh my gosh! Merry Christmas to you both. Merry, merry, Christmas!"

"You two have a lot of catching up to do," John says. "We'll be on our way," he says shaking Mr. Landis's hand. "Thank you both."

"We thank you," Mr. Landis looks deeply and directly into their eyes. "You brought my miracle to me."

"Merry Christmas and God bless you," Sarah adds.

"And to you," Mr. Landis says, placing his arm around his son's shoulder and walking him into the house. He turns and looks at the couple. "Thank you for believing in a crazy man. God bless you both," he smiles, gives them a wave and closes the door.

John and Sarah slowly and silently walk back across the street, noticeably shook up. John stops Sarah when they get to the sidewalk and turns her around to look back at the rooftop tree. "Sarah, look," he points. A shooting star blazes across the sky, leaving a trail. The star on the top of the tree illuminates.

"Oh! Did you see that?" she shouts.

"Yes, I did. I think it's a sign. This is truly your Christmas miracle," he says.

"No," she responds, "It's *our* Christmas miracle. Does this mean that you believe?" she places her hand on his.

"I believe in a lot of things, now," he responds, "thanks to you."

"Oh, I can't take credit for *this*," she replies. "None of it would have happened without you. Besides, there has been more than one miracle this Christmas. I think that I can start believing too. I want to try, John. Will you help me?" she asks.

"Are you kidding?" he gives her a passionate, long kiss. "Merry Christmas, Sarah" John takes her hand. "Come on. Let's go share this with your family!" They both look back at the Landis house. Inside, they see the two men talking and laughing, and hugging.

John and Sarah stop again and kiss deeply before excitedly entering the Wright home. The rooftop tree continues to sparkle against the dark, clear sky.

*Chapter Sixteen*
# Love and Joy

## One Year Later

It is dusk. The rooftop Christmas tree is sparkling brightly. On the front lawn of the Landis house, John and Sarah stand kissing as they embrace. Dozens of people surround them and begin to clap.

"I present to you Mr. and Mrs. Rivera," Judge Conner loudly announces, standing in front of them on a gazebo that is beautifully decorated with hundreds of white twinkling lights woven into fresh, pine roping. White bows and crystals adorn the greenery.

The Landis house in front of them is beautifully decorated and aglow with Christmas lights. The home is newly painted and the lawn is manicured and lined with white folding chairs where a cheering audience sits. Neighbors line the sidewalk and crowd around the beautiful display and ceremony. The rooftop tree casts a beautiful glow over the lawn and guests.

On the porch stands Mr. Landis and his son along with Sarah's Dad, Mother and brother all dressed in formal attire. Mrs. Costello sits in a wheelchair laughing and clapping. Everyone cheers, shaking hands and hugging one another. Judge Conner turns around and looks at Mr. and Mrs. Wright and gives them a "thumbs up." Mr. Wright returns the "thumbs up" as Mrs. Wright blows him a kiss.

The crowd rushes to congratulate the bride and groom. Sarah and John hold each other and kiss once again as they are surrounded by well wishers and family.

"Merry Christmas darling," Sarah sweetly whispers.

"Merry Christmas, Mrs. Rivera," he holds her close and they both look up at the rooftop Christmas tree with huge smiles.

The street scene is a happy one with family, friends, and neighbors celebrating. The small, bungalow homes that line the street are decorated beautifully like any other year with a noticeable difference. Brightly decorated Christmas trees sit atop each of the roofs including the Wright home. The star on the Landis rooftop Christmas tree blazes brightly. A shooting star sweeps across the sky above it.

*THE END*

CPSIA information can be obtained at www.ICGtesting.com
Printed in the USA
LVOW07s2317031114

411894LV00001B/135/P